Miss Green Eyes

By

Kara O'Neal

A Wildflowers of Texas Story

Miss Green Eyes, 1st Edition

Copyright © 2024 Kara O'Neal

Published by Kara O'Neal

This is a work of fiction. Names, characters, places and occurrences are a product of the author's imagination. Any resemblance to actual persons, living or dead, places or occurrences, is purely coincidental.

Not one portion of this work was AI generated.

Also by Kara O'Neal

Gamblers & Gunslingers
Katie's Gamble
Felicity's Fortune
Cora Lee's Wager
Olivia's Treasure
Joetta's Legacy
Everleigh's Game

Texas Brides of Pike's Run
Saving Sarah
Welcome Home
The Sheriff's Gift
The Cowboy's Charms
The Miller Brides
The Soldier's Love
Love's Promise
Love's Redemption
The Editor's Kisses
The Ranger's Vow
The Cowboy's Embrace
Destiny's Secrets
Mr. Pierce's Hero

The Christmas Bride
Maggie's Song
The Inventor's Heart
The Deputy's Damsel
An Unacceptable Wife
The Cowboy's Bride
The Princess's Knight
Sunshine's Welcome
Forever Home

Wildflowers of Texas
Miss Green Eyes

Watch for more at www.karaoneal.com.

Corpus Christi, 1903

Annalee Gillespie has had her world shaken. Her father has died, leaving her as the sole owner of the Circle G. But when the will is read, she's given the shock of her life. She must make the trek up the Chisolm Trail with her foreman, the most irritating man in creation, and complete the tasks given to her, or control of the Circle G falls into another's hands.

Ewan Judge, while capable, smart, and *frustratingly* handsome, has needled and teased Annalee throughout the years, but *somehow* she has to learn to get along with him. He is, annoyingly, the best cowboy in Texas. So, she accepts the challenge and finds herself in the midst of more than one enemy.

A salute to those who are good at small talk...and those who are masters at avoiding it.

Chapter One

Corpus Christi, Texas
October, 1903

Annalee Gillespie paused outside the law office of Peter Jacobs and let out a slow, steadying breath. This was the last task to complete. Once this was finished, she would be running the Circle G all on her own.

Tears pricked her eyes at the reality, and she lifted her handkerchief to carefully wipe them away. Her heart burned with grief.

Her father was gone. He wasn't coming back.

The weight that had lodged in her chest at 3:06 PM on September 28th had not lessened. Not even a bit. She was alone now.

She'd lost her brother six years ago, then her mother three years ago, and now...her father.

And she was responsible for their ranch. The Circle G.

Ten thousand acres.

Over seven thousand head of longhorns.

Twelve tough, calloused cowboys.

One stubborn chuckwagon cook.

One sweet housekeeper.

And...one *frustrating, arrogant* foreman.

Who was probably already inside, because his horse, the great red beast, was already tethered to the hitching post.

After taking a deep breath, Annalee continued down the boardwalk, going past the powerful steed, and the animal twitched its ears. With a soft, watery smile, she turned, then reached over and patted his neck. "Hey, there, Red. You be good, hear?"

The horse snuffled, as if chuckling at her order. Which was exactly what his master would've done. Only he wouldn't have stopped there. He would've added something about her being too big for her britches by trying to be boss.

Annalee shook her head, then reached for the knob to the law office. She gave the grimy, brass fixture a turn, then yanked open the door.

"Oh, good," Peter said, "you're here."

If she enjoyed the company of Ewan Judge, she might've suggested they hitch up the buggy and ride together. But she didn't like to be within one hundred yards of him, so...they'd arrived separately.

She avoided making eye contact with the tall, broad foreman who leaned negligently against the wall to her left, one booted foot braced against the wall, with his thumbs hooked around his belt loops.

"I apologize if I'm late," she said to Peter, her voice cloudy with the tears she'd been shedding.

He shook his head, then scrambled around his desk littered with stacks of papers to pick up a pile of folders from the lone chair. "Not at all," he assured her. He jerked his chin at the tattered, green, leather seat. "Rest yourself."

Smoothing her hands down her dark brown, twill cotton skirt, she accepted his offering.

"And how are you, Annalee?" Peter asked as he searched for an empty space to put down the papers he carried.

Devastated. But there was no reason to say that out loud as it was probably obvious. "I'm fine, thank you."

With his forearm, he pushed a stack of files over, then set his burden down. "I sure am sorry about Jack. He was a good man. The best of us all."

Yes, he had been. "He was the best father a daughter could ask for." Her heart squeezed, and she held her breath as tears threatened. She folded her hands in her lap, pressing her handkerchief between her palms, and doing everything she could to keep from breaking down again. She needed to get this over with.

"Still can't believe that fever got him. Glad no one else on the Circle G got sick." Peter reached over and grabbed a folder that sat on top of one of the stacks. "I've got the information right here. This should be quick."

One would think, but she wasn't sure why Ewan was here. At her father's funeral two days ago, Peter had informed her that he had her father's will and that she and Ewan Judge ought to come down to the office on Monday.

If her sadness hadn't been so consuming, she might've had the forethought to ask why Ewan needed to be present.

But she hadn't. So here they both were.

Peter ran a hand through his thinning blond hair, then sat. He opened the file and perused the contents. Silence descended on the office while the lawyer read quietly.

As the seconds ticked by, Annalee felt the presence of Ewan only five feet behind her. She pressed her lips into a thin line and kept her spine straight. What was he thinking?

Did he doubt she could handle running the ranch despite her father's praise to the contrary? Would he stress that "Knobs", the nickname he'd given her that fateful day so many years ago, didn't have the mind or the courage to hold everything together?

She felt his eyes on her back, which only caused her to want to squirm, but she held fast to her composure. There was no reason to give him ammunition to whatever he already thought.

A lock of her black hair fell from her bun and tickled her cheek. She reached up and pushed it behind her ear.

Behind her, Ewan shifted, the sound of his boot hitting the wood floor.

"Sorry, folks," Peter murmured, his attention solely on the paper he held. "Should've read..." He trailed off.

When he didn't finish, Annalee frowned. Was something wrong? Peter's eyes were slightly wide, as if the information he was taking in was unusual.

Annalee bit her lip, wishing she had experience with wills and inheritances. She had no idea how to assert herself in this sort of situation. Planning a cattle drive she could do. Deciding on what sort of stock to buy was also a strength of hers. She could also analyze the market and could make determinations on what price their cattle would fetch before the men got the animals to the stockyards or railheads.

But *this*...transferring an inheritance...taking the needed steps to be the boss of a ranch...it was foreign. And something she would give anything not to be doing.

Because then her father would be alive.

Jack Gillespie.

The person who, alongside her late mother, had sheltered her, raised her, and educated her. He'd been everything. And now she would have to go forward without him.

Which meant *Annalee* would be the one dealing with Ewan Judge. *If* he stayed, that was. She knew other outfits would like to hire him. He'd never entertained the other offers, because he'd cared about her father too much. He'd started working on the Circle G when he was sixteen. Annalee had been twelve then.

Now, she was twenty-two and was going to be in charge of one of the more lucrative ranches in South Texas. She took a deep breath, then let it out slowly.

Peter cleared his throat nervously, pulling Annalee from her thoughts.

"Well," he started, then paused. He glanced at Annalee then looked past her at Ewan. He twitched his lips, set down the file, and started again, "Um...so..."

Annalee furrowed her brow. Something was wrong. "What is it?"

"Ah...well..." He scratched the back of his neck, then shifted in his seat. "It...ah...seems that your father made some...stipulations."

Stunned, she reared back. "What do you mean?"

Peter looked at Ewan again, then back at Annalee. "I'm just gonna read this, then there's a letter for each of you."

With a nod, disquiet curled in Annalee's stomach. What had her father done?

After clearing his throat, Peter picked up the paper and began.

"I, Jack Gillespie, being of sound mind and able body, set forth this will and testament of my intentions for the Circle G ranch founded by myself and my late wife, Mrs. Roma Gillespie, in August of 1877.

It is my wish that all land, stock, buildings, and other assets be given to my daughter, Miss Annalee Gillespie."

There was nothing odd in that, Annalee thought. She'd known he was going to leave it all to her. He'd told her so, which is why she'd been at his side for the last three years.

Peter glanced at her, then back at the will and continued, "However, her inheritance is contingent upon her completing a set of tasks. The reasons for these tasks are outlined in the letters, one for Annalee, and one for Ewan, that I'm including with this here will and testament. What I assign must be completed by the deadline, or the ranch falls to the supervision of Peter Jacobs for a period of six months. Upon completion of the said six months, Jacobs will decide who is better to run the Circle G, being either Annalee Gillespie or an outside person who has the means, experience, and want to purchase the spread.

The tasks I give my daughter must be supervised by Ewan Judge, my foreman. Upon completion of everything, there is a final prize from which both Annalee and Ewan will benefit.

I affix my name on this day, February 22, 1901, and will carry this to my lawyer, Mr. Peter Jacobs for his witness."

The lawyer lowered the paper and silence fell in the room. No one moved a muscle.

This *couldn't* be right. It just *couldn't*.

Tasks? What tasks?

And she would have to complete them under *Ewan's* supervision?

Annalee closed her eyes as anger throbbed inside her. Her heart roared in protest. She pressed her fingers tightly together, cutting off her circulation.

The silence stretched, crackling with tension. Her contentious relationship with Ewan was well-known, which was why Peter had hesitated so many times before reading her father's will.

"Annalee," Peter ventured.

She bolted to her feet, cutting him off. "You said there was a letter?"

With a sympathetic expression, Peter nodded slowly. "One for each of you." He set down the will, then picked up two envelopes. He held them out.

Annalee took hers, turned away, and opened it.

Ewan's heavy, steady bootsteps could be heard behind her, but soon she was lost in the words of her father's final communication.

Miss Green Eyes,

I'm sorry you're reading this because it means I'm gone from you.

Tears flooded her eyes, and she pressed her handkerchief to her trembling lips. She shuddered on a silent sob. Several seconds passed before her vision was clear enough to continue.

I suppose Peter's read my will to you, and I bet it was a shock. Don't worry, Green Eyes, the tasks aren't difficult. Each one is designed to show you something more about the trail life. Ewan's got to go with you, honey, because I wouldn't want you going alone, and Ewan's your foreman.

I suspect you'll get everything done in no more than two weeks and the six-month trial won't be necessary. I just wanted to give you a little support now that I'm gone. I know you don't like Ewan much, but he's a good man. Trustworthy, strong, smart, and honest. If you seek his help, it'll be solid.

I love you, Annalee. No daughter coulda made a father prouder.

Always,

Your papa

She swallowed a hard lump of aching sadness, then folded the letter. As she gently wiped the wetness from her cheeks with her handkerchief, she grew aware of the silence behind her.

A few beats passed as she gazed out the window, seeing nothing.

So much had changed. So much more was going to change.

And she couldn't stand here forever.

She turned and faced the lawyer and her frustrating foreman. "My letter didn't contain any instructions," she said, her voice raw with grief.

Ewan shifted.

She gave him her full attention.

His black hair fell over his forehead. His stubble framed a sharp, strong jaw. His deep brown gaze snared her with a direct but watchful gleam. "Mine did." His gravelly tone spoke of his own difficulties with recent events.

She knew how much he respected and cared for her father. She was sure Jack's death hadn't been easy on him, either. She raised her brow. "And?"

"We've got to leave in the morning. We're going to Sinton."

"Then?"

Ewan curled his hand around his belt, while he held his letter loose at his side. "We pick up something from the railhead there."

"And is that it?" she asked. "Just one thing to do?"

"I don't think so," Peter inserted, standing behind his desk with his hands in his pockets. "Jack left me several letters that I was instructed to mail the day after his death." Peter shook his head. "I didn't know what was in them, but after reading his will, I'm sure they've got to do with you and this...journey he's sending you on."

She twitched her lips. "Can you tell me how many letters you sent?"

"Seven."

Thoughts swirled in her mind. "So...perhaps we're going to seven different locations on the Chisholm?"

Ewan nodded slowly. "Makes sense."

All right. She could do this. She'd always wanted to make the trek along the Chisholm, but railroads had made the long cattle drives from the early days unnecessary now.

"We can't go by train," Ewan inserted. He lightly shook his letter. "We've got to go by horse."

Of course. Her father wanted her to experience as much of the Chisholm as possible. "And are we sleeping on the trail, as well?"

Ewan inclined his head. "Yes."

Well...this was going to be a bigger journey, but she'd slept on the range plenty of times. She could handle it. "Sounds like we have some preparations to make, then." She turned to Peter. "Is there anything else?"

"Not that I know of."

She had a thought. "Do you know what the prize is at the end?"

Peter shook his head, then gave a hesitant grin. "But it'll be nice to be surprised, don't you think?"

Maybe. She gave him a quick smile in return, but the corners of her mouth trembled. Before she could break down, she said in a shaky voice, "I'll just go on home, start getting ready." She walked to the door, not wanting to talk to Ewan at the moment, but at some point they'd have to speak to make sure they were prepared for the morning. "Thank you, Peter."

"You're welcome," he called to her as she yanked open the door and headed outside.

Once on the boardwalk, she hastened to her horse. The tawny beast waited not far from Ewan's mount.

With trembling fingers, Annalee unwrapped the reins from the hitching post. "Come on, Epona," she said softly, shakily. "Let's go home."

Epona turned her head toward Annalee as she climbed into the saddle.

Annalee knew Epona sensed her upset. "I'm sorry, girl. I'll be all right."

She clucked to her and tugged on the reins to turn her away from the buildings lining the main road that ran through Corpus Christi. She put Epona into a lope.

But it wasn't to home she went. She couldn't.

When the road leading to St. Patrick's appeared, she directed Epona toward it and went toward the familiar, comfortable building. She reined in and tied Epona to the iron fence surrounding the graveyard.

Quickly, as fast as she could, as if she needed to get there before weeping, she went through the gate and hurried to the fresh grave beside her mother's and brother's.

Once there, she sank to the earth and the tears came.

SHE MOURNED. FOR EACH of them. For as long as she dared.

And then...

She got to her feet, brushed off her skirt and let out a steadying, accepting breath. She could now move on until the next wave of grief hit her, then she'd allow herself a moment.

Grief she understood. She could manage it.

It was this...*journey* she wasn't sure about.

But it had to be done.

She turned toward the gate, took one step then halted in her tracks.

Ewan was bracing his forearms on the fence, watching her.

How long had he been there? If the past twenty minutes hadn't been private, she was going to tell him exactly what she thought of that.

Setting her jaw, she started briskly toward him.

He straightened as she got closer. When she reached him, he quirked his lips at her. "I know that look. I'm in for it, aren't I?"

His dry tone irked her, but she refrained from being baited into scolding him over it. "How long have you been here?"

He shrugged. "Just a few minutes. I stayed behind to talk with Jacobs." He glanced over her shoulder toward the graves. "Came here to pay my respects before heading home."

Could she believe him? She never knew if he was telling the truth when it came to their...banter. He always seemed to be teasing her through veiled comments and slightly mocking looks. When he'd called her Knobs all those years ago, she'd declared war, and he'd been very willing to charge headlong into battle. Neither had surrendered.

"That's kind of you," she replied, though her tone carried a trace of doubt. Not about him wanting to pay his respects, but about how long he'd been there.

He made no comment about her suspicion and silence fell between them.

A breeze came through, pulling at some locks of her hair. She pushed her handkerchief into her skirt pocket and let out a sigh. She looked toward the road, thinking about what her father had charged them with. "So...we're traveling companions."

"Seems like it."

She twitched her lips. "I'm sorry. I'm sure you'd rather not go." She forced herself to meet his always confident gaze. "There's nothing in it for you."

"That's not true. Apparently there's some sort of surprise at the end." He gave a slight grin, then made a dismissive gesture with a hand. "But that doesn't matter. Your papa asked me to escort you, and I'm gonna do that. You'll be safe with me, Annalee."

That she knew. The tales she'd heard about his bravery and strength should be written in one of those dime novels. "I appreciate it. I'd rather not have Peter questioning my decisions for six months, and I'm sure he'll be uncomfortable doing so."

"He said as much when I spoke to him." Ewan removed his hat, and the sun shone off his raven hair. He checked something on the brim of his white Stetson, and continued, "I'm sure this journey isn't gonna be difficult. Probably the hardest thing will be sleeping on the ground."

And being in close proximity to him, but she kept the comment tightly reined. "I've always wanted to ride the trail. Papa told me it wasn't necessary, especially since we don't have to drive cattle as far now that trains reach farther."

Ewan put his hat back on. "He's granting you a wish. Hopefully, you'll enjoy yourself."

As long as *he* didn't bait her, she would. Their interactions the last several days had been more subdued. He hadn't teased her once. But, then, her father had passed away. It would be disrespectful to irritate her on purpose. Besides, she knew he was grieving, as well. "I'm going to look at this journey as something to treasure. I'm sure you're right and the tasks will be simple."

"I've been thinking about the seven letters Jacobs had to send," Ewan said. "There are seven stops along the trail that are in Texas, and after the seventh you're in Oklahoma. I'm bettin' our trip stops at Fort Worth."

She perked up at that. "That's where Papa and Mama were married."

Ewan lifted his brow. "Oh, yeah?"

She nodded, excitement filtering through her. "Do you think there would be time for me to visit the church?"

A gentle light entered his eyes. "If not, we'll make the time."

Confused by the softness of his expression, she didn't immediately respond. After a beat, she cleared her throat and said, "Thank you. I wouldn't want to go all the way up there and not see where they were married."

"Never know when you'll be back," he added.

She nodded, then quickly covered any possible awkward silence with, "I'll head on home now and start packing."

He moved to the side so she could push through the gate. "You'll be all right?" he asked her.

"Of course." She gave a quick nod of her head in goodbye, then turned away. As she walked to Epona, the animal heard her approach and lifted her head from eating the soft grass near the fence. Once mounted, Annalee spared a look at Ewan who still stood in the same spot.

That gentle expression on his face was gone and had been replaced with the teasing one she knew so well. "Don't fall off," he warned her.

Irritation spiked within her, but she refused to answer back. She lifted her chin, tugged on Epona's reins then kicked her into a gallop.

Fall off!

When had she *ever*?

He was impossible!

Chapter Two

The following morning, Annalee met Ewan in the yard in front of her house. He'd saddled Epona for her, and her horse waited patiently. He was already astride Red and had the leading string for the pack mule tethered to his horse.

As she mounted, she tried to ignore the man who sat strong and tall atop his steed. The rising sun was displayed behind him, shining around him as if his form was beloved. It was ridiculous how gorgeous he looked.

Ewan was born for the work of drover. Annalee was certain he was riding a horse before he took his first steps.

"Ready?" he asked her once she was settled in the saddle.

She nodded, then scanned the flat prairie, stopping briefly at the bunkhouse where the remaining cowboys would be preparing for a day of moving cattle from one pasture to another, repairing fences, and breaking horses to the saddle. The day-to-day running was being left in the hands of Scratch Scruggs, a man Annalee trusted implicitly.

"Annalee," Delly Scruggs, Scratch's wife, called from the front porch.

Annalee looked toward the woman who was now hurrying down the porch steps with something in hand. Annalee realized what Delly was carrying and wondered how she could've forgotten it.

Delly reached her, her dark eyes filled with encouragement. "You left this."

"I'm so distracted," Annalee said softly. She didn't want Ewan to overhear. She took her bible from Delly and slipped it into one of the pockets of her saddle bags.

"Remember what you said last night," Delly advised. She fiddled with the button at the top of her blouse. The white linen made her dark skin glow. "Keep it at the front of your mind."

Annalee nodded slowly. She'd stayed up late with her housekeeper, lamenting what she was going to have to do and with who and discussing how she was going to get through it. "Thank you, Delly."

The older woman gave her a supportive smile. "Be safe."

Annalee pressed her lips together, drawing on her friend's hope that all would be well. "We'll see you at the end of the month."

With that, she clucked to Epona and reined her around toward the gate of the Circle G.

Ewan followed, the pack mule trailing along after him.

Once on the road, she and Ewan cantered side-by-side, saying nothing. What was there to say? They weren't friends.

But she did plan to use this trip to strengthen their working relationship. She had to set aside past hurts and form a productive partnership with him, which meant she couldn't avoid him as she usually did.

It would be foolish to ignore him. She was aware of how adept he was at being foreman, and he was only twenty-six years old. It could take a man much longer to rise from cowboy to trail boss. But her father had seen something in him and had moved him to the position when Billy, their previous foreman, had been shot and killed in Wichita.

Ewan had been twenty-one at the time, and Annalee remembered her shock at her father's decision. Of course, her dislike of Ewan had run deep, just as it did now, but she had been sure the older cowboys would've balked at having to answer to Ewan.

But that's not what had happened. They had seemed to expect it. Even Scratch had been happy.

As the years had gone by, it had become apparent to Annalee that Ewan was smart, willing to put everyone else first, and had good instincts about cattle and people. She'd had to admit to herself that her father had been right. But she'd done so silently, of course.

After putting some miles behind them, they slowed their horses to a walk, giving the animals a slight respite.

"There's a creek up ahead. Red's gonna go straight to it." Ewan leaned over and patted his horse's neck. "He can ride the Chisholm blindfolded."

Annalee smiled. "He's a good horse. I'm glad he's got colts. We wouldn't want to lose him entirely when the time comes."

"We'll make sure to get more," Ewan assured her. "Best thing is to increase your remuda with stock you already know and trust."

"I agree." She let out a breath and gazed over the terrain. Flat fields of short prairie grass were dotted with Red Oak, Beech, and Texas Mountain Laurel trees. They would bypass the road that took travelers to Corpus Christi and would continue northwest to reach the town of Sinton.

"Texas Mountain Laurel is a pretty tree," she commented, doing what she'd promised herself last night. She was going to try to have a polite, civil relationship with him.

"Especially in the spring when their flowers bloom. Lyle likes to sleep in their shade."

"Oh, yeah?"

Ewan nodded. "He says they give the coolest cover."

She hadn't known that about the older cowboy. "Does he miss the long cattle drives of his youth?"

With a shrug, Ewan said, "I'm not sure. There are things to miss about them, and things to be glad about."

"Such as?"

He cleared his throat. "Things to appreciate would be the drives aren't as long and are safer. We're home more often. I know some of the younger fellas are glad, because they feel they can get married. Things to miss are not seeing the sights, getting out and being gone. When you're on the trail, you meet others and now we can't commune with friends from other outfits as often."

"Y'all could write letters," she offered.

Ewan laughed. "Naw, that's not something a man usually does. He might write his mother, or his father, but not another fella."

"Maybe that's *your* preference. My father wrote letters all the time. Some of them were to friends." She had spent time with him while he'd worked on his correspondence.

"He had to do that, because it was important for him to keep up relationships with the other cattle barons."

She frowned but kept her gaze on the trail ahead. "I didn't perceive all of his communication like that. He was friends with many people."

"I'm sure he was friendly with a lot, but one thing you gotta know is that cattle barons are always looking to increase their stock and their rangeland. They'll go after a lame duck in a second."

That gave her pause, and she whipped her gaze to his profile. "Will the Circle G be seen as such?"

It was a moment before he turned to meet her gaze. "Yes."

She nibbled on her lower lip, then focused back on the horizon. An incline was before her, and she recognized it as a possible dip to a creek. But her mind was on what Ewan had confirmed.

She fell silent, worried that she would have to contend with cattle barons who thought they might be able to talk her into selling. Or worse, sabotage the Circle G so she was *forced* to sell.

Epona sensed the water and jerked her head.

"Come on, girl," Annalee said softly. "Let's take a rest."

"This way," Ewan said, leading the way slightly to the left, probably to a good spot on the bank for horses to drink.

Once the animals had their heads bowed to the stream, Annalee dismounted and stretched. She tried to ignore the anxiousness in her stomach.

A Live Oak grew along the bank, and she went and leaned against its trunk.

Ewan was busy making sure the supplies were still tethered good to the mule.

She watched him, admiring his form. He was a handsome man, and everyone's favorite on the ranch. Except hers, of course.

But his popularity was why his teasing hurt so much. Everyone liked him and listened to him. As a young girl, she'd been no different. She'd been so desperate for his approval and attention. Then at a social, when she was fourteen and he eighteen, she'd accidentally elbowed him in the stomach while dancing with someone else. He'd doubled over, trying to catch his breath, then had called her Knobs. In front of *everyone*. She bit her lip and looked away, gazing out over the creek.

"Thirsty?"

She flinched, not having heard him approach her. When she turned, she saw he was holding out a canteen to her. With a quick smile, she took it. "Thank you."

"No trouble." He turned and looked out at the horizon.

As she lifted the nozzle to her lips and took a drink, she tried to settle her nerves. She'd never been alone with him. Not like this. There was no one else around, and it was as if they were the only two people on earth.

After taking a few sips, she screwed the cap back on, then passed the canteen to him.

He took it with a slight quirk of his lips. "Got enough?"

"Yes, thank you." She turned her attention to the horizon, noting the position of the sun. It was around ten in the morning. They would be in Sinton by noon, which would allow them to eat in town if they chose.

"Are you thinkin' on how the other cattle barons are gonna treat you?"

She should've been. Instead, she'd been agonizing over his nearness. Because—and she *hated* the realization—she found him attractive. When he wasn't talking, she could imagine that he was a gentleman. His masculinity rolled off him, and she wasn't immune to his effect. She cleared her throat. "I'm worried about it, but I don't feel like I can concentrate on it until I begin making decisions. I'm aware of the meeting in November with all the cattle barons in South Texas. I've met several of them over the last few years. I'm anxious to meet Henrietta King of the King Ranch."

Ewan gave a slow nod. "Good woman. And she manages a big outfit. You should have a friend in her."

Would this be a good time to ask him what he thought about her as a leader? Or should she leave it be? Her father had put her in charge, and *he* had believed in her. *That* should suffice. Her nerves settled at the last thought.

"So..." Ewan said, breaking into her reverie, "you're sittin' all right in the saddle."

Her hackles rose slightly. "Did you think I wouldn't? You've seen me riding the range."

He shrugged. "It's not the same. Those are short distances from one pasture to the next."

She twitched her lips, trying not to let him get to her. His comment had been somewhat of a compliment. "I suppose riding the trail is different."

"It's about the length of time. Your body might get sore."

When she felt him glance at her, she turned her head and caught the wry grin on his face. She drew in a sharp breath, bracing herself.

"Especially since you're all knees and elbows," he said, his gaze twinkling.

The most embarrassing moment of her life came rushing back, and she went ramrod straight. "Ewan! I swear you are impossible!"

He chuckled. "I still have the bruise."

"You do not!"

His grin got wider. "Sure do." He patted his stomach.

She stamped her foot. "Why do you keep bringing this up? And if that name you call me passes your lips *one* time, I swear I'll—"

"You'll what?" he challenged, a heated light in his eyes. "I'm not afraid of you, Knobs."

Knobs!

She took a step forward and shook her finger at him. "I could fire you!"

He laughed outright. "That would be the outside of stupid. Everyone would think you'd gone mad."

"Well! As your boss, I demand you never refer to that moment again, nor will you call me that name. Never again!"

"Just keep your elbows away from my gut, and we'll be all right," he drawled, not bothered at all by her anger or threat.

Firing him would be stupid. She knew that. But it was all she had. She set her jaw and tilted her chin up. "It's time to go. We need to be in Sinton by noon." With that, she stormed around him and went to Epona.

He was impossible!

"THE TRAIN DEPOT IS this way."

Without comment, Annalee followed Ewan at a trot, allowing the mostly empty streets and buildings of Sinton to distract her. For the last two hours, she'd kept her statements to him at a minimum. When he'd asked her a question, she'd responded without looking at him.

Which was childish, she knew, but she was too angry and being barely civil was the most she could do for him. She let out a breath and prayed that she could make it through this trip without firing him. She needed him.

And, of course, there was the danger that he would quit, especially if her childish behavior grated on him. Somehow, she would have to stop caring when he teased her. That was her only recourse.

When they reached the depot, they tugged their horses to a halt. The platform was empty. The window for the ticket counter was open, though.

Ewan dismounted, so she did, as well.

She wasn't sure what they would be given. Another set of instructions according to Ewan, and she imagined he was right.

With a nod at the counter, Ewan said, "You go on up. This is for you. I know Bud, and I promise he's gonna prefer to see your face over mine."

She lifted her brow but made no comment. As she moved toward the window, her boots scuffed on the wood platform.

Someone within cleared his throat, then hollered, "Be with you directly. Got a situation."

As she waited, she heard the man wrestling with something. Had to be an animal. The interior of the ticket booth was too dark for her to see the inside, and the window was too small.

"Get out, you ornery critter!"

The sweep of a broom and howl resounded, then the flash of a light as a backdoor was opened then shut quickly.

"Damned infernal thing," the ticket taker groused.

A flash of red to her right caught her eye, and she chuckled to see a fox racing away.

"I'm comin'," the gentleman called as he slammed the backdoor. "Trains are runnin' steady today." His boots scuffed on the wood floor. "Where're ya headed?"

When he appeared, and she got a look at him, she instantly knew who he was. Her heart leapt in gladness. "Are you Blackie?"

His gray brows lifted. "Only one person calls me that and I got a letter that he died." He leaned forward and his perpetual black eye was even more present. "I'm thinkin' you're his little girl."

Annalee pressed her hands to her chest. "I am, and I've wanted to meet you for a long time!" she exclaimed.

"Meet me? What fer?"

She couldn't help but grin. "Papa told me so many stories about you. I think you're a really fun person."

His suspicious attitude changed to a cocky one. "Oh, yeah?" He grinned flirtatiously. "Why don't we go dancin', then? You stayin' long?"

She laughed in delight, recalling the tales her father had told of his friend Blackie, who always had a black eye for his flirting and wily ways. He proposed at least once per week to females who came through town. Depending on how he asked, his urgings earned him a punch to the face by either the woman or the man escorting her. Sometimes his assaulter was a husband. "Well, I—"

"We're just here for the letter Jack left for us, Bud," Ewan drawled. "No more, no less."

"You hush up, you runt," Blackie shot back, looking over Annalee's head. "We're chattin', and the lady can answer for herself."

Annalee snorted, then covered her mouth.

"See there?" Blackie continued. "She doesn't want you 'round neither." He turned his attention back to her and turned on the charm with his smile once more. "Whatcha say, girl? We'll do some boot scootin' at Charlie's, and I'll order you a nice steak dinner."

She pulled a mock frown. "No proposal? You have to try me out first before you ask?"

His brow hit his hairline in surprise at her comeback, then he laughed robustly. "Darlin' girl, if'n I thought you'd say yes to an old codger like me, I'd a already asked."

She chuckled, then said, "I'm mighty glad to meet you, Blackie. I begged my father for stories of you whenever he'd get back from a drive."

"Glad I brought you some happiness." He reached over to the counter to his right. "I'm real sorry your pa is gone. He was a good 'un."

"Yes, sir." The pang of remembering sliced at her but didn't make tears smart this time.

He handed her an envelope. "I was told to give this to ya. Don't know what it says."

She read her father's bold scrawl, noting that he'd addressed it to her and Ewan. "Thank you." She pressed her lips into a thin line, then nodded at the colorful Blackie. "I hope I see you again some time."

He gave her a lazy salute. "I'm always here."

After giving him a nod of goodbye, she turned and held out the envelope to Ewan. "It's addressed to both of us."

He slipped his hands into the pockets of his denims. "You can open it."

She stepped closer to where the horses and mule waited as she rent a slit in the envelope. Her heart pounded slightly, wondering what the instructions would be. If the rest of this journey allowed her to meet people she'd always wanted to know and visit places she'd always wanted to see, it might not be so bad. She just wished Ewan wasn't the person with her.

After withdrawing the letter, she unfolded it. Seeing her father's bold scrawl made tears prick her eyes. Quickly, she blinked them away and took a deep, steadying breath. She read aloud.

"My little Miss Green Eyes,

Guess you made it to Sinton. Knew you would. Especially with Ewan as your escort. Hope you got the full force of Blackie's charms, and he had his signature black eye.

From here, y'all need to get to Beeville. You'll find your next letter at the Trenton Hotel. The lobby attendant should be taking care of it. Your next set of instructions are waiting for you.

Always,

Your papa"

She ran her gaze over the letter, drawing in his words and missing him, her mother, and brother so much. Except for the snuffling of Epona, silence surrounded her.

After a few moments, Ewan said gently, "I'm sorry, Annalee."

His tone of compassion washed over her. She appreciated his sympathy, and the urge to comfort him came over her. She lifted her head and looked at him. "You love them, too." Ewan would know she referred to her whole family.

He nodded slowly, his gaze intent upon her. As it usually was. "I do," he said.

Her heart tugged, and she found herself unable to look away from him. His eyes shone with so much feeling, but about what she couldn't discern. What she saw was more than just his sorrow over what they'd lost. It was as if...

But...no. It couldn't be.

She blinked and took in a breath, breaking the connection between them. Swallowing hard, she looked over her shoulder toward the main part of town. "Should we find some place to eat and then press on?"

"Sure."

Why was his tone raspy and filled with some kind of meaning?

Her heart skipped a beat, and she was transported back to when she was twelve and had been so enamored of him. She'd made it her mission in life to get his attention, to impress him and make a friend of him.

But all her hopes had been destroyed when he'd doubled over in agony after her elbow had connected with his stomach. Those around them had laughed, and he'd teased her about her gangly limbs. That's when she'd realized what he'd really thought of her.

"Ready to go?" he prodded, sounding more like himself. "I know a good café."

She shook out of her memories. "Yes, I'm ready."

Without words, they mounted up and turned their horses and the mule toward town.

Chapter Three

A fire crackled at the campsite they'd made halfway between Sinton and Beeville. The air was slightly cooler, proving they were moving north.

Annalee sat near the dancing flames, sipping water after taking a refreshing swim in the nearby creek. She'd washed her hair and felt clean after the long day of riding.

Ewan was pitching her tent for her. He'd offered, telling her they should share the camp duties.

She'd made him a meal of beans and cornbread. Of which he'd had thirds.

He'd taken care of the stock while she'd cooked, and they'd done everything in companionable silence. It should've been odd, but no.

Perhaps having tasks had kept any awkwardness at bay. Or perhaps she was starting to let go of the past.

She hoped it was the latter.

His boot steps came closer to the fire, and his tall frame appeared in the orange light. "All done," he told her. He was carrying the needed tools to hammer the stakes into the soil. "Hope you don't mind, but your tent's only about a foot from mine."

Her stomach dipped and swirled with the news, and she gripped her tin cup more tightly. "That's fine. I understand why that's necessary and appreciate your care for my well-being."

He quirked a grin and gazed at her for a few moments.

"What?" she prodded, knowing that teasing glint in his eyes.

With a shrug, he replied, "Nothin."

She twitched her lips. Should she let it go? If he was choosing not to tease her, shouldn't she be pleased? But...her curiosity got the better of her. "No, tell me. What's got you grinning like that?"

He let out an indulgent sigh, smoothed a hand over his stubble, then acquiesced. "Sometimes I feel like I ought to bow before you. You've got this way of talkin' that's fancy."

He didn't like the way she spoke? Well! She wasn't surprised. He found most things she did to be odd anyway. She gestured with her hand. "By all means, then. Please. Bow after I say something to you. I am your boss, aren't I?"

He chuckled low in his throat. "Yeah. Gonna have to get used to that."

She lifted an eyebrow at him. "Don't expect my help."

He snorted, then laughed. "Never thought I'd get it, and that's all right. If you can learn not to get your dander up every time I'm around you, it'll be fine."

"Stop bothering me like you usually do, and I won't snap at you." She lowered her lashes and took a sip of her water.

When he didn't reply, she looked at him. He was studying her with his usual amused, crooked grin.

"Well?" she prodded. "Do you think we can get along without your mockery of my ways and words?"

He let out a breath, then shrugged. "I'll try."

Stunned, she reared back slightly. She hadn't expected him to agree. She'd asked him to stop teasing her many times, but he'd never relented.

He lifted the tools he held. "I'll just put these away."

She bit her bottom lip as he walked toward the stock.

Maybe things were gonna be all right. Maybe they *could* have a polite working relationship. The next year was gonna be difficult, and she needed him.

She...needed him.

She paused as a wave of emotion gripped her. Struck, she pressed two fingers to her temple and rubbed. What were these feelings? Why...

With force, she shook her head and pushed to stand. She didn't need *him*. She needed his *expertise*. Her feelings were mixed up because she was tired and sad and anxious.

After stowing the tin cup in one of the bags, she strode to the horses. She found him speaking softly to Red, and the sight made her heart flip. Annoyance spiked, and she clenched her jaw against the ridiculous flutters inside her.

Ewan lifted his head. "Somethin' wrong?"

"I'm just gonna turn in."

"Oh, sure. I'll take care of the fire."

"Thank you. Good night."

"Night."

His parting reply followed her as she walked away, and while she was able to put distance between them, the image of him speaking in hushed, gentle tones to his horse was at the front of her mind.

A dangerous image to carry around.

It had taken her several years to let go of the tender feelings she'd had for him as a young girl. She'd fancied herself in love with him for a time. She couldn't go back to that, especially since she had other things to worry about.

Once inside her tent, she got as comfortable as she could, wearing her chemise and single petticoat. She laid down in her bedroll and stared at the darkness.

Too much was on her mind. Too much was not settled.

She was not going to rest.

Closing her eyes, she sighed in despair as worry reigned.

THEY ARRIVED IN BEEVILLE by noon and rode straight to the Trenton Hotel. In sync and in silence, they tied their horses and the mule to the hitching posts, then Ewan held the door open for her so she could enter.

A front desk was directly in front of her, while a singular staircase that split at a halfway point to the right and left rose behind the desk.

A brown-haired gentleman in a three-piece suit with a full beard and spectacles, worked behind the counter. He was bent to a ledger, writing carefully within its pages. He looked up.

Annalee smiled at him. "Good afternoon."

"Howdy," he answered, removing his spectacles. He must not need them to see her. "Welcome to the Trenton."

"Thank you." She could feel Ewan's solid, steady, and quiet presence behind her. It was comforting. Which was unfortunate.

She shook off her dismay and smiled at the attendant. "My name is Annalee Gillespie, and—"

"Oh," he broke in, "I have a letter for you."

"Yes, I was told you would."

"Odd thing," he said, as he leaned down to find it within the storage of the front desk. "But my manager said he knew your father well and wasn't bothered by keeping something as important as mail." He rose and handed her the envelope. "Hope it's what you needed."

"Thank you." She stepped away and opened the letter as Ewan held the door open for her once more.

On the walk in front of the hotel, she quickly scanned the contents, and her heart leapt with joy. "Oh, Papa, you're going to grant all my wishes, aren't you?"

"What's it say?" Ewan asked, looking over her shoulder.

His warmth seeped into her, and she had to work to keep from shifting nervously. "He's ordering us to attend a play at the Grand Opera House."

"Oh, yeah?" Ewan's tone conveyed his own delight. "That's nice. Wonder what's playing."

She turned to face him but made sure to put a little more distance between them. "He says we will stay the night at the Trenton, attend whatever show is playing, then leave for Luling in the morning. We're supposed to find the next letter at the feed store."

Ewan's brow lifted. "He must want you to meet Mrs. Finch."

Which was another one of her wishes. The woman had decorated her husband's feed store with images of finches, and apparently the building could be seen a mile outside of town.

Was this journey supposed to teach her something? While she was learning how to get along with Ewan, the tasks she was being given weren't about the ranch. Not really.

Why would her lawyer have to supervise her for six months if she didn't manage to get to the final stop in time if all she was doing was having fun?

"You seem confused," Ewan commented.

She let out a breath. "Well...it's just that these tasks don't seem necessary." She waved a hand. "I mean, I'm excited to attend the opera house, and I loved meeting Blackie, but why did I need to do this? Was it really just to experience the trail? Am I not going to have to make difficult decisions?"

With an uncertain hand, Ewan smoothed his stubble. "Ah...well..." He cleared his throat. "Maybe the final stop will give you answers to your questions."

There were four more destinations after Luling. He could be right. She nodded. "Yes, that's possible. I'm sure there's a point to all of this. Papa wouldn't have me doing this if it weren't important." She gave Ewan a quick smile. "Let's get rooms, shall we? And I'll need to visit the mercantile. I don't have a thing that's good enough to wear to an opera house."

He grunted in acquiescence as he followed her back inside.

After securing rooms and giving their bags to a bellhop, Ewan suggested stabling the stock at the livery, then finding a café.

Annalee agreed.

It didn't take much time to find the livery, and while Ewan spoke with the operator, Annalee waited just outside the open double doors. She wasn't too far from the school and smiled at the children playing in the yard. Their happy squeals made her heart squeeze in longing.

She yearned for her own family, for the opportunity to be a wife and mother, but that would have to wait. For many reasons. Sadness gripped her, and she forced herself to turn away from the children.

Ewan emerged from the livery at that moment.

"All done?" she asked quickly, trying to ignore the pangs of grief plaguing her.

His brow knitted. "Uh, yeah."

"Good. Let's go eat." She turned on her heel, going to the left where most of the buildings sat along the main road.

He fell into step beside her. "Are you all right?"

"Of course." She suppressed a wince at her too bright tone. "I'm looking forward to this evening."

"The livery operator told me that *A Doll's House* is playing at the Grand, and he also said that there's a decent restaurant in the hotel." He gripped her elbow as he guided her onto the road so they could cross to the other side.

"He was quite helpful then," she squeaked out. Ewan's solid, protective hold only made the sadness she was trying to ignore grow.

"Are you sure you're all right?" he asked, his gaze on her profile.

She kept her focus straight ahead. He was too close to her. If she turned her head, she knew his enigmatic gaze would ensnare her, and she couldn't risk that. Not when her feelings were so raw. "I'm fine, I assure you."

He didn't respond but did turn his too keen stare away from her.

When they made it to the hotel, and he let go of her, she let out a relieved breath as discreetly as she could. She was going to have to build thicker walls to protect herself from his handsomeness and capability, or the rest of the day and the evening ahead, were going to be difficult.

ANNALEE CHECKED HER reflection in the standing, oval mirror in her room. She'd found a pale pink, silk evening dress at the mercantile. She'd had to take it in an inch at the waist, but the length had been perfect. A series of vertical tucks lined the bodice, curving nicely over her breasts. The cap sleeves were edged with lace, and the square neckline showed the barest hint of her cleavage.

The skirt fell softly around her legs and was embellished at the bottom with the same lace that edged the sleeves. A modest train completed the ensemble. It was delicate and not overly done. She liked it very much.

The color made her cheeks glow, her raven locks shine, and her green eyes that her father had loved so much, to sparkle. She felt beautiful.

Ewan would probably ask her if she was enjoying playing dress-up.

She let out a breath and closed her eyes, scolding herself for creating arguments that hadn't happened. So far, he'd been a gentleman more often than not. She needed to stop assuming he was always going to find a reason to tease her.

Besides, she was going to an opera house for the first time ever. Her father was granting her a wish, and it was making her feel as if he were close. How wonderful!

With her heart pounding in anticipation, she left her room. She came to the stairs and descended, scanning the lobby for Ewan. She frowned when he was not in sight. He'd said he'd be waiting for her. Was she late?

She reached the bottom floor, concerned. Reaching up, she fiddled with a tendril of hair framing her face.

Heavy boot steps to her left caught her attention, and her heart leapt in feminine appreciation when she saw Ewan looking forbiddingly handsome.

He wore a new suit with a black coat, burgundy striped vest, white shirt, and a black tie. His hair had been trimmed as had his beard. His appearance was hands-down gorgeous, but his smile was what truly had her pulse racing.

"Ewan," she breathed when he reached her.

"Evening," he said in a low, intimate tone. "You look beautiful."

Her cheeks heated, and her mind went to mush. "Thank you."

He jabbed over his shoulder with his thumb at an open door. "I was getting us a table at the restaurant. I'm sorry that I made you wait."

She swallowed the lump of awe in her throat and tried to get control of herself. "No harm done."

"Good." His smile softened. "Wouldn't want to upset you."

At his tender expression, her heart pounded even faster and harder. "You didn't."

His gaze gleamed with heat, and he nodded slowly. "I'm glad. Can I escort you into the restaurant?"

Such a kind, polite request. And he'd complimented her appearance. And his tone was gentle, almost a caress upon her skin. *What* was happening? "O-Of course."

He offered his arm.

She looked down at it, her breathing going shallow and her heart beating at an uncontrollable rate. What had she thought no more than a few hours before? That she had no feelings for him? That she'd lost that girlish fascination she'd once held for him?

Tentatively, she set her fingers in the crook of his elbow, realizing she'd been wrong.

When his free hand came over to cover the tops of her fingers, as if he wanted to hold her close, she bit her lip and worked hard to keep from looking up at him. She didn't want to see what was in his eyes.

If it was teasing, knowing mockery, her heart would break.

If it was invitation, promise...*caring*, she would melt into a puddle at his feet.

No. She would *not* look at him.

He led her into the restaurant and straight to a table. He helped her sit, then took the chair across from her.

The dark walnut paneling and low light from the brass sconces made the space more romantic than she was prepared for. She had to get control of the feelings overwhelming her. She just *had* to.

Quickly, she set her napkin in her lap, then unfolded her menu. She perused the offerings, but the words blurred before her. Her body cried out to meet the gaze she felt upon her face.

But she was terrified to do so.

She *couldn't*.

A waiter came to fill their water glasses. When he asked if they wanted wine or other alcohols, she refused. Ewan ordered three fingers of whiskey.

She kept her focus on her menu, silently begging her heart to settle and her mind to work. The silence between them stretched, and she had to resist the urge to squirm under the tension.

"You're studying the food pretty hard," he commented.

Why did his voice wash over her and seem to be pulling her to him? She swallowed. "I can't decide."

"Steak is always good." He shifted in his chair, the wood and leather creaking beneath his weight.

"I believe I'd prefer fish tonight." Was that squeaky tone really hers? What was *wrong* with her?

"Are you all right?"

She *had* to behave normally, and she had to gather her wits from wherever they'd gone. Firming her resolve, she closed her menu and as she set it on the table, she forced a smile at him. "Just fine. I'm looking forward to the play. Do you know anything about it?"

With a dubious light in his eyes, he shook his head slowly. "I've never heard of it. I've only been to one play before."

She latched onto that bit of information like a bird snatched up a worm. "Oh? What was it?"

"Don't recall the name. Saw it at the opera house in Luling. Something about the devil tempting some fella."

"Did you enjoy it?"

He nodded. "Yeah. It was a first for me. I was with your father and a few of the other hands. They'd threatened to hogtie me and drag me to it if I didn't agree to go."

She furrowed her brow. "You didn't want to go?"

With a rueful quirk of his lips, he shrugged. "I don't usually partake in town events. I prefer the peace and silence of the range at night."

That was news to her, and she was surprised. "I didn't realize that. Papa's stories of the fun y'all had always included you."

"He made me go."

"Why?"

Ewan waved dismissive hand. "He said that I needed to experience life and that cows couldn't provide a man any caring."

His cheeks had gone ruddy. Was he embarrassed about something? The haze of attraction and desire finally lifted from her, and she felt her pulse slowing down. Still though, she was tuned to him more than any other person she'd ever known. "You don't like to be around people?"

"No, I do. I'm just...uncomfortable during the initial meeting. I'm not good with small talk." He shifted in his chair, as if he was bothered by his weakness. Or perhaps he didn't like admitting it to her?

She wanted to put him at ease. "I completely understand. Living on the ranch, so far from town and from other girls my age, made it difficult for me to learn how to make friends. I'm grateful we went to church every week. It took time, but the more I practiced, the better I got." She smiled encouragingly.

His mouth quirked at the corner, and his embarrassed expression changed to one of soft fondness. "So...I should practice more, huh?"

Why was he looking at her like that? Was he going to tease her again? She pushed away her niggling worry and replied, "Sure."

"With who?" He held out his hands. "It's not like we're going to any parties where we need to socialize with others."

She sat straighter in her chair. "Well...with me then."

"You?"

Thinking about her idea, she grew more sure of her suggestion. "Yes. We don't really know each other, do we? I mean we've ridden the range together, but that hasn't allowed us to delve into each other's personalities and past history." This could be good. This could help her understand him better. She knew next to nothing about his childhood.

He cleared his throat, a veil of doubt in the sound, then shrugged. "All right. What should we talk about?"

How interesting. She'd learned that he could get nervous. *Him.* Everything in her eased and loosened. "If you start your conversations like that, I can see why it's hard for you."

He lifted his brow. "How should I start?"

"How about with a question that tells you where the person grew up?"

"But I know where you grew up."

She rolled her eyes. "It doesn't have to be that one, but something similar."

He made a noise as if he was slightly irritated.

Their waiter came with his shot of whiskey.

"Thanks," Ewan said, "I certainly need this."

And while she chuckled, he took a sip.

The waiter took their order for their meals.

"All right," she continued after the server had left with their food choices, "go ahead and ask me something about my life."

He rolled his tongue against the inside of his cheek as he thought. "How about...who's your favorite hand on the ranch?"

"That's not a question I should answer," she told him. "Now that I'm the boss, I can't have favorites."

Ewan let out a breath of exasperation. "Fine, then you do it. Ask *me* something."

"I didn't take you for a quitter." She gave him a pointed look.

"I'm not, but you're the teacher in this exercise. Show me how it's done."

That was fair. She cocked her head and thought for a moment. Not because she didn't know what to ask, but because she had too many and she wanted to pick the best one.

Mentally she discarded several before inquiring, "Did you work on a ranch before you came here?"

Memories shone in his gaze at her question. "No. My father owned a saddlery in town."

"Which town?"

"Burnett."

"Did you help him at all?"

"Never got a chance to. He, my mother, my two older sisters, and my older brother died of sickness when I was four."

Her heart broke for him. "I'm so sorry," she said softly.

He nodded slowly. "Yeah."

The ease she'd found with him was now thickened with sadness. But that was a risk when getting to know someone. "What happened to you?" she asked hesitantly.

"Went to live with another family. They owned the newspaper, and I started making deliveries when I was six."

"Were they kind to you?" she asked as heartache gripped her on his behalf.

He gave her a look. "*This* is small talk?"

She flushed. "I-I beg your pardon."

Quickly, he waved her off then leaned his forearms on the table and gazed at her intently and with apology. "Don't think on it. Sorry. Just seems we're gettin' a little more personal than if I met someone for the first time at a barn dance or somethin'. I was only teasin' you."

She pressed her lips into a thin line, wishing she hadn't asked the question, but appreciated him trying to make her feel comfortable again.

"And to answer you, yes, they were kind. They had their own children, of course. The business was gonna go to the oldest son, and I wasn't much for writing anyway." He shrugged. "So, I started off on my own when I was sixteen. Came to your pa's ranch by way of an ad he'd put in the paper. He hired me without much inquiry."

"Really?" Intrigued, she leaned forward. "Why?"

"Well, lookee here," a male voice interrupted. "Ewan Judge. How the hell are you?"

Annalee glanced up and found a stocky gentleman with a handlebar mustache, and thick, brown hair striding purposefully toward them wearing a big grin.

"Ewan Judge?" another voice called. It belonged to a tall, lanky man, who was coming up behind the first one. Curiosity and surprise shone in his startling blue eyes.

"Howdy, gentlemen," Ewan said, rising to shake their hands. "How are y'all?"

"Fine, fine," the taller one said. "We've come to town with our wives. Going to the play."

Ewan nodded. "So are we."

"And who is your lovely companion?" the stockier one asked.

"Gentlemen, this here is Miss Annalee Gillespie."

Each man's eyes went wide with pleasant surprise. "Well, how do you do, ma'am?" the stocky one said as he reached for her hand. While they shook, he said, "I'm Gregory Vaughn, owner of the Sweet Creek spread southwest of here. And this is—"

His friend inserted himself quickly, holding out his hand, "Beau Wilton, owner of the Double Bar that's adjacent to Sweet Creek."

"It's very nice to meet you both." Annalee smiled politely as she withdrew her palm from Mr. Wilton's tight grasp. She went back in her memory to recall what her father had told her about them. She remembered that they were decent fellows with ingenious ideas on progressing the breeding of cattle.

"This is quite fortuitous," Mr. Wilton commented. "Mind if we join you for a moment?"

Before she or Ewan could object, they'd each drug a chair over from an empty table. Annalee shared a look with Ewan, and she easily read his annoyance and disappointment.

But she didn't want to send the men away. This was her first introduction to them, and she wanted to learn more about them. However, she *was* disappointed that she wasn't going to continue her conversation with Ewan. It had been nice, and it may not be simple to draw him back in later.

The cattle barons got comfortable, and Ewan resumed his seat.

Then, in a matter of seconds, Annalee found herself wrangled into a deep discussion about breeding her longhorns with their angus stock.

Chapter Four

A *Doll's House* enthralled Annalee. She never once took her eyes from the stage. The main character, Nora, was married with children, and hungry to do additional things with her life. She loved her family but searched for ways to enrich her future further.

It spoke to Annalee in that she was also on the cusp of doing something new, something different. She was going to have to be courageous.

On the walk back to the hotel, she chatted non-stop about the show, and Ewan appeared to be listening attentively. Which warmed and charmed her even more. If not for the tingles Ewan caused to fly over her skin just by being near her, she would call the evening perfect.

How she wished she wasn't affected by him so much, but his handsomeness was too raw and masculine to ignore. She was only a woman and not impervious.

When they reached the lobby, Ewan continued on with her, bypassing the restaurant where Mr. Vaughn and Mr. Wilton had invited him to after the play. They'd wanted to drink the remainder of the night away; they'd declared jovially during intermission. Ewan hadn't accepted or rejected their request.

As they climbed the stairs together, Annalee's anxiety began to increase. She'd never been at her door with a man at the end of a night on the town. She'd heard that sometimes there was a goodnight kiss after such an evening.

But why would he do that? They weren't courting. This outing had been orchestrated by her father.

However, that didn't stop her from imagining the scene. Her mind played out what Ewan might say, what he might do. She could feel his fingers trail along her jaw line, and her heart squeezed in longing.

Oh, good gracious! She *wanted* him to kiss her.

Her pulse began to race, and her stomach was tied in knots. *Oh, heavenly days!* Where was her head?

"I'm glad you had fun," he said in low tones. "I enjoyed it myself."

"Did you?" she replied, forcing the squeak of nervousness from her tone.

"Sure. Especially since I wasn't required to make small talk with anyone." His tone held a vein of laughter.

She let out a breath, wishing she could be as easy with him as he was with her. He didn't seem affected by *her* at all. "We didn't get much opportunity to practice, did we?"

"Vaughn and Wilton lassoed our conversation and didn't let it go, huh?"

They turned left and started down the corridor on the second floor. "They're adamant that breeding my longhorns with their angus will be successful. I'm not sure why they're so interested in my stock."

"Your pa had a reputation for the healthiest herds. We've rarely had sickness take any of them."

Yes, she was aware. She looked ahead and saw they were approaching the door to her room. Her heart leapt into her throat. Surely, there wouldn't be any awkwardness. Certainly, he wouldn't have a look about him that suggested he wanted to kiss her.

Because if he did, and if he tried, she was going to let him. And that just couldn't happen.

"Here we are," she announced in a too bright tone.

"Get some rest," he told her as she removed her hand from the crook of his elbow. "We'll leave bright and early. It'll take two days to get to Luling."

She busied herself with finding her key in her purse. "I'll be ready. Shall we meet in the restaurant for breakfast or," she found the key and inserted it, "did you just want to eat on the trail?"

"It'll be better if we eat in the saddle, if that's all right."

"That's just fine." She unlocked the door and pushed it open. She looked up at him and gave him a smile. "Thank you for an enjoyable evening."

"It was fun." His expression held nothing more than ease and politeness. "I'll see you in the morning."

"Yes, goodnight."

He gave her a lazy salute, then she entered and shut the door.

As she sagged against the panel with her hand still on the knob, she heard his muffled steps carrying him away.

Well...he hadn't looked at all like he'd wanted to kiss her. In fact, she doubted he'd even seen her as a man sees a woman.

Her heart sank to her stomach.

"ALREADY OFF?" MR. VAUGHN asked Annalee as she stood with Epona outside the livery.

"Yes, we have to get to Luling."

"Judge told us your pa is sending you on a little jaunt up the Chisholm." Mr. Vaughn tipped his hat back and smiled beneath his handlebar mustache. "Hope you enjoy it."

"I'm sure I will."

"Have you thought more about our conversation?" he asked her, hooking his thumbs in his vest pockets.

She glanced toward the inside of the livery where Ewan was concluding their business with the owner. "A little. I confess I can't put my mind to it until I'm home."

"That's fair." Mr. Vaughn jerked his chin toward the entrance to the stables. "We said more to your foreman last night."

"Oh?" She furrowed her brow. "When?"

"He met us for drinks after he got you settled. We had a good time."

Uncertainty washed through her. "I didn't realize that he'd gone ahead and met y'all."

Mr. Vaughn held out a placating hand. "Don't fret, Miss Gillespie. Judge never once undermined you. He just listened."

And as quickly as it had come, her unease fled.

"Of course, Wilton offered him a job more than once," Mr. Vaughn revealed with a grin. "You might be careful, Miss Gillespie. I'm thinkin' my neighbor might've made too tempting an offer."

And just like that, her world came crashing down. She gritted her teeth against the hurt and worry gathering inside her. "Ewan has been with us for ten years. I highly doubt Mr. Wilton is going to be successful."

Mr. Vaughn shrugged. "A man's got to go where the greatest success will be. It's the way of things. Loyalty is all well and good, but if there's no possibility to further oneself, why stay?"

His point resonated with Annalee, and she couldn't fault Ewan if he was considering leaving. She supposed more money was one way to measure success, but to her mind, family was more important. And while she and Ewan had always had a tumultuous relationship, he was beloved by everyone else.

Before she could respond to Mr. Vaughn, Ewan appeared leading Red and the mule.

His brow lifted when he saw Mr. Vaughn. "Are y'all leavin' now also?"

"Yep. But we took the stage. Got our women with us, you know." Mr. Vaughn moved away from Annalee to shake Ewan's hand in goodbye.

"Oh, sure. Well, safe travels."

"And to you, as well." Mr. Vaughn turned to Annalee and tipped his hat. "Ma'am."

"Goodbye, Mr. Vaughn." As she watched him stroll away, she tried to control the anxiety still swirling in her stomach despite the logic of his argument. Should she offer Ewan more money?

"You ready?"

Ewan's question distracted her, and she whipped her head in his direction. He was seated on top of Red, looking down at her with an open, easy expression.

She swallowed, then said, "Yes, of course." She mounted up. "Lead the way."

They kicked their horses into a canter and were soon on the trail heading north.

THAT EVENING THEY MADE camp near a lake shrouded by cypress, oak, and dwarf palmetto trees. After preparing and eating a supper of biscuits, beans, and bacon, she washed the dishes in the water. The sun was lowering behind the trees, turning the sky glorious shades of pink and purple.

She put the clean dishes on a linen towel she'd spread on the soft grass and enjoyed the beauty surrounding her as she worked. Sunset was always her favorite time. The still of the evening, the peace, reached deep into her and soothed her soul. The back porch of her home also afforded her a perfect view, and she often ended her night there.

It was where she and her mother had had so many talks, where she snapped beans and shelled peas with Delly, and where she went when she needed a moment with God. Seeing the colors now, intermixed with the green of the trees, refreshed and renewed her spirit.

When she finished the dishes, she wrapped the ends of the towel around the tin, then stood with the bundle in hand. She carried everything back to camp, then slipped the plates and forks into the one of the bags leaning against her tent. She tied the cast iron pan to the outside, then pushed to her feet.

She drifted toward the fire where Ewan rested with his back against the trunk of a Live Oak. His Stetson rested in the grass next to him, and he'd unbuttoned the top three buttons of his blue chambray shirt. He gave her a soft smile. "All done?"

"Yes." She sank to the ground, stretching her legs out in front of her, and after swiping some grass off her brown, twill cotton skirt, she leaned back on the heels of her hands. "It's beautiful here."

He nodded slowly, scanning their surroundings. "That's another thing to miss about long cattle drives. The changing scenery. The Texas landscape is beautiful, and...varied."

"Papa loved it. So did Mama. You know she wrote poetry about nature? I have a whole book of her poems." A precious memory popped into her mind and she grinned. "You know, Ramsey wrote, too."

At that, Ewan let a quick chuckle. "Don't believe it. Your brother wouldn't put pen to paper even if it meant his words would turn to gold."

She laughed. "Oh, yes, he did. I found his poems. He'd left them in the front parlor, and I was half-way through reading them when he caught me."

Ewan quirked an eyebrow at her. "Still don't believe it."

With an emphatic nod, she said, "They were short. Two-line to four-line stanzas that—"

Ewan's brows lifted. "Oh, you're talking about his songs."

She paused, confused. "What do you mean?" she asked after a second.

"He got tired of the songs we'd sing to the cattle, so he started writing his own." Ewan shrugged. "Said "Barbara Allen" was too sad, and "Aura Lee" made him tired. So he took to writing his own."

"I didn't know that." She was pleasantly surprised and began trying to recall some of what she'd read. She squeezed her eyes shut. "Was there one about a lady crossing a bridge because the man she loved was on the other side?" She looked at Ewan.

He nodded. "Yeah. Beth."

"Huh. This is interesting. I didn't know that about Ramsey." And for the first time in six years, she felt as if her brother was close. A thought occurred and her heart leapt in hope. "Can you sing one of his songs?"

Ewan's cheeks went red. "Do what?"

"Sing. One of his songs." She folded her hands and brought them to her chest in hopeful supplication. "Please?"

In a flash, Ewan relented. "All right." But his face got even redder, and he let out a steadying breath.

She didn't want to make him nervous, and she drew breath to tell him he didn't have to, when his voice lifted in a beautiful melody. Her breath caught, and she gripped her fingers more tightly.

The notes of a tale of Beth seeking her true love and building a bridge to get to him were sweet, but it was Ewan's full baritone that put her into throes of almost rapture. His voice wrapped around her, enthralled her, and made her heart pound.

He held her gaze captive while he sang, never once looking away.

How had she never known? How had…

She swallowed and lowered her hands to her lap. His voice was incredible. He was…

Oh, dear. She couldn't finish the thought. Couldn't admit to herself what was growing in her heart. Or, rather, what she'd been ignoring for the past several years.

When he trailed off, ending the song in a way that caressed her skin from head to toe, she had no idea what to say…what to do. She just gazed at him, like a ninny.

He inclined his head toward her and lifted his brow. "What's wrong? Was it that bad? You can't talk?"

Slowly, she shook her head. "No, that was…beautiful." The awe she felt rang in her tone. "I didn't…" She swallowed. "I didn't know you could sing like that."

With a shrug and a bashful expression, he said, "Don't really advertise it. Ramsey knew, which is why he made me learn all the songs he wrote. He was gonna put them in some kind of book."

"Was he?" She barely registered what Ewan had said as her pulse still had an erratic beat. This man had hidden talents, and she was even in more danger of losing her heart to him. What was she going to do?

"Yeah," Ewan continued, "but he never..."

When he couldn't finish what he'd started to say, Annalee snapped out of the spell Ewan had cast over her. Her brother's death had hurt him, too. Ewan was only a year older than Ramsey, and they'd spent a lot of time together while herding cattle.

An ache over what they'd lost centered in her breast. So much had happened in the last six years, starting with the death of her brother. "He'd had such a future ahead of him," she rasped.

"I think about Ramsey," Ewan said, pulling her from her thoughts. "A lot."

"Do you?" Her brother's image appeared in her mind's eye. In her visions, he was always smiling down at her from the saddle.

"I think about things we did together," Ewan went on, "and how he was as much a brother to me as anyone. If I had been there when that bull charged, I would have..."

When he couldn't finish and instead looked out into the distance, she pressed her lips into a thin line. She knew what he was thinking, what he wished, that he wanted to turn back time and change the outcome. Her father had agonized over the same.

After several moments of quiet, she said softly, "It is what it is."

Ewan looked at her, and in his eyes she saw his sadness, his own hurt at the loss of someone he'd cared about.

"If we," she began carefully, "spend our days thinking about what could've been, then it makes it hard to go forward. And it especially makes it hard to go forward happily." She shook her head. "Ramsey, and

Mama, and Papa wouldn't want us to spend our weeks and months and years in a fog."

Ewan swallowed. "I know, but it's hard knowin' that your pa didn't have his son. And that...he had to settle for me."

She reared back, stunned. "Oh, Ewan, no." The urge to embrace him came over her, but she didn't move from her position. "In fact, it's just the opposite. He was so *grateful* he had you."

A pained, sad light shone in Ewan's gaze.

"I promise," she assured him earnestly, leaning forward. "He told me on more than one occasion that he couldn't do anything without you, that he thought of you as his own."

Ewan was quiet for a moment, seeming to take in what she'd said, then he gave her a soft smile. "Thanks, Annalee."

She hoped he believed her. He was as much a part of the family as Delly and Scratch, and all the other hands who worked on the ranch. She couldn't imagine going through life feeling as if you didn't belong somewhere or to someone.

She wanted to say more, but disquiet and uncertainty held her back.

Silence settled between them, and the crickets' song rose, distracting her. She realized the sky had darkened, and stars were appearing.

"About time to turn in, huh?" he said.

She looked at him, and his expression was soft with ease, with...gentleness. And it that moment, she realized just how dear his face was to her. She bit her lip and nodded slowly as dismay gripped her.

She was in love with him. Had always been...in love with him.

And he thought of her as nothing more than...Knobs.

"ONCE WE ROUND THIS bend, you'll get your first look," Ewan told her with a grin as they trotted the remaining mile into Luling.

Eager for a distraction from the upsetting acceptance of her feelings, she craned her neck, searching for the first glimpse of Finch's Feed. As soon as the sharp bend straightened, she saw a roof that appeared to be the resting place for at least one hundred birds. She gasped. "How does she get them to land on her roof?"

Ewan chuckled. "Those aren't real. She made all of those."

Stunned, Annalee reared back in the saddle then looked at him. "You can't be serious?"

"It's part of the oddity. Mrs. Finch has made her husband's store infamous, and people come from miles away. Makes for a lot of business."

Equal parts astounded and impressed, Annalee turned her attention back to the wooden building. A sign with Finch's Feed written in big, black letters hung over the entrance. Three steps led one to the door. More handmade finches rested along the crossbars of the railing framing the porch.

Murals of trees littered with finches had been painted along the whitewashed walls, stretching over the sides and curving around to the front. Annalee was enchanted. It was odd but beautiful at the same time.

As soon as they reined to a stop, she slid out of the saddle and hastened up the steps, eager to meet the woman responsible for such uniqueness. Annalee paused on the porch to get a look at the handmade creatures on the porch railing.

She was surprised to see that Mrs. Finch had not used real feathers but had instead used fabric. She'd painted the material to make the bodies look as if they were covered with feathers. Marbles replaced eyes, while twigs had been used for legs.

The woman was quite talented, because while the materials she'd used could be identified, the birds looked very life-like. It was amazing. Excited, Annalee reached for the knob and entered.

Once inside, her eye was dazzled by more murals and handmade birds. She barely noticed the other customers or the varieties of animal feed and other farming supplies lining the shelves stretching down the center of the building.

She left the door open and began to wander, looking at the murals up close. Forest, garden, barn, river all served as backdrops to showcase finches. Had Mrs. Finch painted every scene? If so, she was amazingly talented.

"Can I help you folks?" a male voice asked, interrupting Annalee's winding walk through the shop.

She turned and discovered Ewan was near the door, with his hand curled around his belt. It appeared he'd been waiting while she'd wandered. How long had she been perusing the murals?

"Howdy," Ewan replied, taking two steps to the right and moving closer to the man standing behind the counter. "My name's Ewan Judge, and this is Miss Annalee Gillespie. We're here—"

"Oh, you're the folks with the letter."

"Yes, sir." Ewan gave him a polite smile. "We were told to come here to fetch it."

Mr. Finch nodded. "Strangest thing. We got mail from Jack Gillespie, asking us to keep a letter for y'all. Only met the man a few times, but I could tell he was an all right fella. He didn't come with y'all?"

Annalee bit her lip as a twinge of sorrow pierced her. She made eye contact with Ewan who wore a sympathetic, soft expression.

"Naw, he's not with us," he answered for her. "We're taking a trip, sort of a scavenger hunt, that Mr. Gillespie created."

The man's gray brows knit, and he replied, "Huh. Odd thing." He let out a breath and waved a hand at the interior of his shop. "But then who am I to call somethin' odd?" He chuckled then shook his head. "My wife's got your letter. Gillespie asked for her to be the one to hold on to it and to give it to y'all. I'll get her. She's in the back."

Mr. Finch walked to an open doorway that appeared to lead to a storage room, then disappeared inside. Muffled voices could be heard.

Annalee folded her hands and rested them against her black, twill cotton skirt, trying to forget why her father wasn't at her side. She shared a soft, quiet look with Ewan, easily reading his own sadness.

"You're here," a feminine voice sing-songed.

Annalee turned and found an older woman wearing a burnt orange, gingham skirt and a blouse of the same color hurrying toward Annalee.

Mrs. Finch's round face was wreathed in a smile. A cameo was pinned to the neck of her blouse, and she'd swept her graying auburn hair into a high bun. "Are you Miss Gillespie?"

Before Annalee could answer, the woman went on with, "Of course, you are." She reached Annalee and took her hands in hers. "Who else would you be? My, you're just lovely. Just as your father said you would be. And look, Mr. Finch, her green eyes do shine bright. I can see why your father calls you Miss Green Eyes."

Annalee's throat instantly went raw with emotion. "Yes, ma'am."

"Such a fitting nickname. Just like the flower with its green center and yellow petals. So pretty!"

Texas Green Eyes. The wildflower that grew in the fields of Texas had been consistently gathered by Annalee's father, put into a bouquet and brought to her when he'd come home from a hard day of work. She still had the very first flower he'd ever given her pressed into the pages of her bible. She'd been five-years-old, and he'd picked the single blossom to show her how pretty her eyes were. She swallowed the lump of sadness sitting at the base of her throat. "Thank you, ma'am."

"I'm sure you're anxious for your letter," Mrs. Finch said. "I have it here." She withdrew an envelope from her skirt pocket and handed it over.

As Annalee took it, she said, "I love what you've done to your shop. You're so talented."

Mrs. Finch's eyes shone with pleasure. "Thank you so much. It took some time, and it needs a lot of upkeep. I have to climb onto the roof," Mrs. Finch linked her arm with Annalee's and began walking her over to a mural of a gazebo with birds flying in the painted sky above or nesting in the eaves, "and it upsets Mr. Finch to no end, but our pets must be taken care of."

"Of course."

"This was my first painting," Mrs. Finch said, then launched into her story and process.

Annalee listened avidly, glad that the woman was so forthcoming. It was interesting to hear about another's business ideas, and she didn't take any bit of it for granted.

Customers came and went as Mrs. Finch showed Annalee every mural and discussed the meticulous process of creating the fake birds. Throughout the half-hour it took, Annalee would check on Ewan. He never appeared irritated while he kept himself off to the side.

"My goodness, I've talked your ear off, haven't I?" Mrs. Finch shook her head at herself.

"Oh, I enjoyed it," Annalee assured her quickly.

"Aren't you a dear?" Mrs. Finch said with a smile. "I'm so glad to have met you."

Annalee was charmed by the woman and replied, "And I, you. I hope we get to talk again some time."

The woman brightened. "That would be lovely. If you ever find yourself in Luling again, come on by. We'll have supper."

As she withdrew her arm from Mrs. Finch, Annalee said, "How kind of you."

It only took a few moments to say their goodbyes, then she and Ewan were outside. "I'm sorry if that took too long." She stopped in the yard, only a few feet from where their horses were tethered.

Ewan shrugged. "I'm fine. I didn't mind."

Many people would've at least been slightly bothered by having to wait, and her heart squeezed with love for him at his show of kindness. She gave him a soft smile, holding his gaze for the briefest of seconds, then she lifted her hand and waggled the letter she was still holding. "Let's open it up."

He nodded once.

After withdrawing the paper with its instructions, she read quickly. When she was finished, she asked, "Our next stop is Lockhart?"

"Should be."

"He says there's no letter there. We just camp there one night, then we're supposed to go on to Austin and stay at the Driskill Hotel. He says we can visit the capitol, ride the streetcars, and visit any other place we might like to go." She folded the letter. "We get to stay two days in Austin if we want."

"That'll be a nice rest. I've stayed at the Driskill before. It's quite a hotel."

"Papa told me, and I begged to see it." She slipped the paper back into the envelope. "He's granting me so many wishes." A sudden thought occurred, and tears pricked her eyes. "Do you think he wanted this for me as a way to find comfort since I would be all alone?"

It was a moment before Ewan said in low tones, "Maybe." He paused. "But you're not alone."

Her breath caught. What did he mean? Did he intend to be, at the very least, a friend to her? The possibility thrilled her clear through, and she fell into his warm, brown eyes, into the care she saw there. Her pulse raced as something rose between them. The silence stretched with an intimacy, a sharing that sent her heart into all sorts of flutters.

He cleared his throat and looked away, as if self-conscious. "Want to go into town and find a place to eat and sleep?"

Why did he seem embarrassed? Had she imagined the feelings between them, or had her own expression made him uneasy? Her heart dropped to her toes, and she rasped, "Yes. That would be fine."

With no more than a nod, he moved away from her and went toward his horse.

Dismay gripped her, and she followed him.

Well...

She'd always known he didn't have feelings for her. She was "Knobs" to him. Not a woman. A child with nothing more than elbow, knees, and a clumsy gait. A future with him was hopeless.

Chapter Five

The Driskill Hotel was like nothing Annalee had ever seen. The main doors opened into a lobby that stretched as long as the entire block. The tiled floor was inlaid with beautiful golden and navy accents and supported columns that were intricately carved. The luxury of the columns rose to the ceiling which showcased paneling also done in navy and gold, and a stained glass, flipped dome lit by electric lights.

A wide set of stairs led to the rooms and broke to the right and left at the midway point. Plush carpeting, electric lighting, and carved, cream-colored paneling decorated the corridors.

The hotel sported a luscious bar, a restaurant done in fine linen, crystal chandeliers, and mirrored walls, lavatories with bathtubs, electric fans in every room, and a bank. It was decadent.

But she could find no awe, no pleasure, no joy in being able to fulfill another of her wishes granted by her father. Agony was twisting in her heart, slicing at the very marrow of her bones, and stealing any peace her soul could find.

She was in love. Unequivocally. Unceasingly.

All these years, she had ignored it, covered it with anger and hurt, pretended she couldn't care less about him to save her wounded pride. But now, after spending days and nights with him, after being consistently bombarded by his face, his form, his capable hands, and his calm, quiet, steady nature, she was helpless. She could no longer lie to herself.

And he did not love her back. He felt nothing but polite consideration.

Ever since the moment outside Finch's Feed, he had not made direct eye contact with her. He'd spoken to her only when absolutely necessary.

It was pure torture, and she was going to have to live with it for so long. How would she manage to get over him? Especially since he worked for her. And not only that, he was her foreman.

As she paced her room, she agonized over what to do and what her future held. Loneliness for certain. It wasn't as if she was often around men similar to her in age and situation. It was a ten mile ride to Corpus Christi from the ranch, and she usually only went into town on Sundays.

But she couldn't even think of falling for someone else. She wanted *Ewan*. She *loved* Ewan.

It was unbearable.

She let out a shuddering breath, unwilling to let tears fall. She was supposed to meet him in a few minutes to read the letter they'd picked up from the lobby attendant when they'd checked in. From there, he was going to take her to see the capitol building. They were even going to take a tour.

Pressing a fist into her stomach, she closed her eyes and forced herself to breathe steadily.

Once she had relative control of her emotions, she went to the washstand and checked her appearance.

Her blue lace blouse complimented the umber color of her twill cotton skirt. The black belt at her waist helped show off her figure, and her dark locks glistened in the electric lights coming from the brass sconces.

She turned her head from one side to another, assessing her face. Her parents had always told her she was pretty, but she really had no way of knowing if that were true. Her eyes were, indeed, a striking green. Folks often complimented the color.

A wave of sentiment gripped her, and she went to where she'd laid her bible on the night stand next to her bed. She flipped it open to the spot where she kept items that meant much to her.

A scripture, written by Delly, and given to Annalee on the day of her brother's funeral. A letter written to Annalee by her mother and given to her on her sixteenth birthday, and finally, a wildflower wrapped in a linen handkerchief.

Annalee carefully lifted the top fold of the handkerchief and gazed at the Texas Green Eye placed there. Its yellow petals were a golden-brown now, and the green center wasn't as bright as it had been all those years ago. But it was *her* flower. Her very first one. Given to her by her father to show her how bright her eyes, how lively, how sharp.

It was a moment she'd held close over the years, and she was grateful she'd taken care of the treasure.

Her father had always told her to be as free as the wildflowers. They grew where they wanted and when they wanted. They weren't considered as fine as roses, but did that stop them from growing? Didn't they still blanket the fields of Texas, showing the world they were meant to be there?

Yes.

And so should Annalee do.

Somehow.

A knock sounded, and she jumped.

But the sharp rap hadn't come from the main door, but a side door she hadn't noticed. Hesitant, she closed the handkerchief with careful fingers, then shut her bible.

Another knock came, and she set her bible on the side table then rounded the bed. When she answered the summons, she was surprised to see Ewan on the other side.

He lifted one eyebrow. "Seems our rooms are connected."

Her heart leapt into her throat. "Really?" She glanced over his shoulder and saw a similar furniture arrangement as her room.

"Want me to go down and ask to move?"

She swallowed, then did her best to slow her racing pulse. "No, no. How is it any different than when we're sleeping in our tents on the trail?"

He paused, thinking about her point. After a moment, he inclined his head. "You're right. There's no harm in this, either. Besides, I need to be close so I can protect you if something happens." He gave her a quick, encouraging grin.

His acceptance and analysis of the situation only made her feel more desolate. And why? Because she *wanted* her nearness to be a problem, to be an agonizing torment like his was to her.

My goodness, she didn't understand herself. She cleared her throat and tried to appear unaffected. "Thank you for considering my safety."

"My pleasure."

"Are you ready to head down?"

"Sure. We can take a streetcar straight to the capitol. Have you got the letter?"

She slipped her hand into her skirt pocket. "Yes."

"All right, well," he grinned at her, "let's go." His gaze gleamed with excitement.

His expression made her center clench in longing. This was unbearable. She gave him her own smile. "Yes, let's." She turned, and he followed her through her room.

She picked up her purse, then once they were in the corridor, she withdrew her key. After locking the door, she pulled her father's letter from her skirt pocket. As they walked, she read silently. When she was done, she said, "We go to Waco next. The letter is with the priest at St. Mary's."

"We aren't supposed to visit anything else?" Ewan asked as they reached the stairs.

She shook her head. "He didn't say to."

"Huh."

As they descended in sync, she could hear him thinking. She wondered what he thought of this trip, if he minded escorting her across Texas.

She should ask, she thought. But only if she wanted more heartache, because certainly he would say he found it irritating.

They reached the main doors, and he took her by the elbow. "Here, this way."

He led her to a streetcar stop on the corner, and they only had to wait a few minutes for a car to arrive. Though she had seen the contraptions when they'd first arrived in the city, she was still amazed by them.

Once aboard, she was able to forget her unrelenting, unrequited love for the man sitting next to her. There was so much to see. Stone and brick buildings rose four and five stories high, while wide and columned bridges spanned the river running through the city. Some shops had clock towers on top of their roofs, and when she saw black lamp posts lining the main streets, she realized they were electric.

The capitol building was impressive with its dome, but even more beautiful was the Goddess of Liberty that sat on top. She held the sword of justice in one hand, and a gilded lone star in the other. So much work had gone into the structure.

Annalee's eyes remained wide as she took the tour of the capitol, and when they left, she couldn't help but exclaim her delight. On the ride back to the hotel, she couldn't stop talking about all the sights.

Ewan never once asked her to take a breath. He didn't even appear bothered.

Music reached her ears, and she looked in the direction of the sound. A small building with wood walls was to her left, and she read its shingle as they passed by. "The Scoot Inn." Through the front windows she saw dancing couples. "Oh!" she gasped. "A dance hall!"

"Yeah, many of the boys have visited that saloon."

Annalee whipped around and folded her hands, holding them to her chest in supplication. "May we do so? Could we go? What's it like?"

Hesitancy shone in his eyes. "Ah, well, I'm not sure we should. I've heard it can get rowdy."

"But you'll be there with me, and I'm sure it's quite safe. There were other women inside." She'd never been to a dance hall. Barn dances, yes, but not to an actual assembly room with a bar.

The reluctance in his gaze only got sharper, and he pressed his lips into a thin line.

Suddenly, she realized that if they attended, he'd have to dance with her. They couldn't go and just stand on the sidelines. She instantly sobered. "I'm sorry. You're right. We don't have to go."

He opened his mouth to speak, but then paused, as if he wasn't sure how to respond.

Seeing how reticent he was, only sent a knife slicing into her heart. She had no wish to spend an evening of dancing with someone who had no want to partner with her. She simply had to convince him she was fine with not going. "There's no reason to invite any trouble, and who knows what we might encounter. I'd rather not cause you any problems."

He swallowed. "I'm sorry, Annalee. I just don't think it's a good idea."

She held up a staying hand. "It's fine. Please don't worry."

With a slow nod, he fell quiet.

She turned to look out the window and fought tears of heartache.

THE FOLLOWING DAY, Annalee and Ewan visited gardens cultivated near an underground spring and a river. The beauty did much to distract her from her current sorrows. She even thought more on partnering with Mr. Vaughn and Mr. Wilton and breeding her longhorns with their angus stock.

She had some references she wanted to check when she got home, but she was leaning toward agreement. She'd go over the process with Peter, her lawyer, and meticulous contracts would have to be drawn up. But she was warming to the idea of doing something different with her stock.

When they returned to the hotel, a gentleman in a three piece suit and flat-crowned hat was standing near the stairs. His face broke into a smile when he laid eyes on Ewan. "Well," he drawled, "Ewan Judge. How are you, young fella?"

Ewan stuck out his arm and shook hands with the man. "Just fine. Didn't expect to see you here."

The gentleman jerked his chin toward the outer doors. "Just come from registering a new brand. Bought the Split Hairs Outfit."

Surprise shot through Annalee. That spread was not too far from her own. Why had Jim Cook sold?

"Good for you," Ewan said, but his own tone rang with some hesitancy. He turned to Annalee. "Let me introduce you to Miss Annalee Gillespie, Jack's daughter. Annalee, this is Buck McCauley."

Sympathy passed over Mr. McCauley's face, and he held out his hand for her. As they shook he said, "I was real sorry to hear about your father. Good man. Good, good man. Damn good cattleman."

"Thank you, sir." Annalee remembered that Mr. McCauley ran a rather large spread in south Texas. The Two Bar X. And now he'd bought the Split Hairs. Again, Annalee wondered what had made Mr. Cook sell.

"You folks stayin' the night?" Mr. McCauley asked.

"We are. Leave for Waco in the morning."

Mr. McCauley's brow lifted, and he smiled. "Then we could spend supper together, if'n you didn't have other plans."

Annalee shared a look with Ewan, and his gaze asked her for acceptance or rejection, and because she was interested in what happened with the Split Hairs outfit, she turned to Mr. McCauley and replied, "That would be fine. Is seven agreeable?" That would give her some time to freshen up.

"That's mighty fine. Mighty fine."

She gave Mr. McCauley and Ewan a soft smile. "I'll see y'all then. I'm going to head to my room to rest."

Ewan nodded and Mr. McCauley tipped his hat.

As she ascended, she could hear the men's low tones as they continued their conversation, but she felt Ewan's gaze on her back. She wasn't sure why his focus was still on her when he should be giving Mr. McCauley his full attention. Perhaps he was just making sure she made it to the second floor. He was, to a fault, treating her safety and comfort as utmost importance.

Once alone, she gathered the toiletries she needed, then went down the hall to the lavatory. She was going to have a nice soak, take a nap, then have a clear head for her conversation with Mr. McCauley.

A LIGHT KNOCK ON HER door had her checking the time. It was a quarter to seven. She quickly finished rubbing lavender scented hand cream into her fingers and palms, then went to answer the summons.

Ewan was there, and her heart flipped at the sight of him. He'd changed into fresh black trousers, a dark green vest, white shirt, and black tie. With his black hair, brown eyes, and stubble covering his jaw, he looked forbiddingly handsome. "Did you rest?"

"I did, thank you." She smoothed the sides of her bun and hoped her plum tea dress, cinched at the waist with cream lace, made her beautiful. She *felt* beautiful, and she was going to believe that she was, she thought decisively. With a slight lift of her chin, she asked, "Shall we?"

"Yes, but in a minute." His expression had turned serious and cautious.

Taken aback, she didn't reply for a moment, then stepped aside so he could enter. She shut the door, then turned to face him. "What is it?"

He pressed his lips into a thin line and after a few silent seconds revealed, "McCauley's gonna ask if you want to sell."

"*What*?"

Ewan nodded slowly. "He told me he had an offer for you and asked if I thought you'd be open to it. I told him he had no chance, but he's still gonna ask."

Struck and flabbergasted, she put her hands on her hips. "My father is barely gone, and Mr. McCauley believes I'm ready to hear offers for my ranch?"

With a shrug, Ewan replied, "That's not gonna matter to a businessman. His job is to make a profit. He must be in a good position to be able to buy another spread after just securing the Split Hairs."

As her mind swirled with thoughts, she began to pace slowly. "He must think I feel overwhelmed, and the Circle G is close to the Split Hairs. And *his* ranch is in south Texas, as well. He must want to connect his range land."

"That's a smart assumption."

Disbelief coursed through her at what was ahead for her tonight, and she shook her head. "I can't fathom this, but I'm not going to sell. I have no intentions of ever doing that unless there's no other recourse." She stopped pacing, faced Ewan, and with a joking tone said, "I could very well send us all into the poor house in less than a year, though."

Her statement fell between them, and he frowned as if he disapproved of it.

He straightened. "You're not gonna do any such thing. You're smarter than you realize."

Awed, she could only blink at him. She hadn't ever expected to hear him compliment her like that. Her heart squeezed in equal parts joy and sorrow. How she loved him, and how she wished he loved her back.

But now was not the time to let her yearning for him take over.

She swallowed. "Thank you, but I'm well aware that a cattle baron is only as good as the people working for her. And I know that you're the best in the state, Ewan." She recalled the offer he had from Mr. Wilton, but quickly shoved it out of her mind.

Ewan's cheeks went ruddy. "Thanks."

A charged silence grew between them, and she stared deep into his eyes. She could look at him forever. If he'd let her.

Mentally, she shook out of the spell he'd cast with just his gaze and let out a steadying breath. "Let's go."

He nodded once.

After locking her room, she took his arm, and they proceeded down to the hotel restaurant without speaking. When they entered the dazzling space with its linen tablecloths, crystal chandeliers, and cream paneling, she immediately saw Mr. McCauley.

The man was rising to his feet from a round table near the bar. He wore a big, cheshire grin. "Evenin', folks."

"Good evening," Annalee responded while Ewan pulled out her chair. She sat, then reached for her menu. She sensed Mr. McCauley's anticipation and confidence as he shook Ewan's hand. She wondered why he seemed so sure of himself. Guards rose up inside her, and her mind sharpened.

The men sat, Ewan with silent assessment and Mr. McCauley with jovial excitement.

"What's good?" Mr. McCauley asked as he snapped his linen napkin open.

Annalee smiled at him over her menu. "I'm sure all of it is."

With a grin, Mr. McCauley lightly banged a fist on the table. "Then let's have it all."

She laughed like she wasn't suspicious of his confidence. "I'm afraid I would not be able to indulge to that extent."

"Oh, you must have *something* decadent, Miss Gillespie," he argued lightly. "Let's see." He looked at his menu. "Hmm. Oysters might fit the bill. Or maybe the marinated fruit and cheese?"

Ewan waved a dismissive hand. "I'll be fine with just steak and potatoes."

"And I think the roast will do for me," Annalee announced.

Their waiter came and they ordered. Mr. McCauley went ahead and asked for both the oysters and the marinated fruit and cheese.

Once the waiter had left, Mr. McCauley set his elbows on the table and leaned slightly forward. "So, Miss Gillespie, has it sunk in that you're the boss now?"

The question readied her for the conversation coming. Beside her, Ewan went a little rigid, but she doubted Mr. McCauley could tell. Ewan kept his emotions under tight control and only those who were used to his ways would detect his simmering anger.

"Truthfully? No." She gave the man a slight shrug. "But my father's only been gone a little over a week. He spent three years, the years after Mama died, teaching me everything I would need to know, and I have the best foreman in the state, so..." She held up her hands. "I'm not worried."

A veil of challenge rose in Mr. McCauley's eyes. "And you're prepared for this ever changing business?"

"As prepared as I can be."

"And the dangers? Have you thought about them?"

As Mr. McCauley began to grill her with question after question, Annalee's anger grew little by little. He boldly ran an inquisition: Was she ready to handle the moods and ways of the cowboys? Could she handle discussions with veterinarians? Was she ready for auctions and did she know how to properly assess good stock?

Had she learned about the innovations with the equipment used for housing livestock, feeding them, and herding them? Would she be able to do business with railroads as their owners liked to drive up prices for hauling steers?

He did not let up. After every answer she gave, he had another question ready. She understood what he was doing. He was trying to scare her, to make her doubt herself.

But the more he tried to back her into a corner, the calmer and surer she became. He was not going to frighten her out of her birthright. Not only had her father intended for Annalee to have the ranch, if she sold, that would mean all of the cowboys and Delly's future would be uncertain. She would *not* sell her *family*.

After a good hour had passed, she set down her fork on her empty plate and said, "I believe you've questioned me about every aspect of the ranching business. It's been quite extensive. I'm not sure why you felt the need to do so."

His cheeks were high with color, and he wore a forced smile. "It's a tough enterprise. Need to make sure you're ready."

"That's not your responsibility. That belonged to my father, and I believe he did a thorough job."

Mr. McCauley shrugged, took a final swig of his whiskey, then set the glass on the table. "Time will tell, Miss Gillespie. Time will tell."

Silence fell between them, and she shared a quick look with Ewan. His eyes told her it wasn't over. She waited.

"But you know," Mr. McCauley went on, twisting his glass on the tablecloth, "seems to me you may not want to work so hard. A woman like you...I bet you'd prefer to be a wife and mother. Hard to do when being a boss of a ranch."

She inclined her head. "I would adore being a wife and a mother. I hope God leads me to that vocation."

His gaze sharpened as he seemed to sense an opening. "Then perhaps you should consider selling your spread to me. You'll have a hard time managing things, and I'm prepared to give you an offer that's fair."

Was he? She had to work to keep from scoffing.

"Also—"

She held up her index finger, and he stopped.

She held his gaze, allowing blessed silence to reign, and considered her response carefully. After several moments, she said, "Mr. McCauley, I have no interest in selling."

His eyes widened a fraction.

"There isn't an offer you could make that would convince me to sell my home. Not only would that shame my father, it would be disrespectful to his and my mother's memory. Additionally, selling my ranch means abandoning the family I do have."

He twitched his lips and held himself very still. "Sentiment is a poor reason to run something you won't be able to handle."

Anger shot up her spine, but she refused to let him see. She lifted her brow. "I'm not selling, Mr. McCauley." Her voice rang with finality.

He pursed his lips as he glared at her, studied her.

She felt his thin control and knew he wanted to argue further, so she waited patiently. She did not break eye contact with him.

Finally, his shoulders slumped, and he gave a rueful grin. "Can't blame a fellow for tryin'."

"Of course, not. I'm not bothered by you asking. I'm aware that this is business and not personal."

"Wonderful," he said cheerfully, "then let's have a toast to our future dealings and put this out of our minds, shall we?"

She inclined her head.

Mr. McCauley looked over his shoulder toward the bar, and he signaled the gentleman working there with a slight whistle.

The man in white shirtsleeves and a red vest glanced up as he cleaned a glass with a towel. "Sir?"

"Three glasses of champagne, please."

"Of course."

When Mr. McCauley turned around, he switched his avid attention to Ewan and instantly drew him into conversation about an acquaintance's health.

She was relieved and let her focus wander. The mirror behind the bar allowed her to see most of the room and the bartender as he filled three glasses with bubbling champagne. She watched the golden liquid rise to the halfway point of the crystal.

When the bartender reached for a small brown bottle, she cocked her head. *What's that for?*

He poured the contents into one of the glasses, then carefully lifted the flute and swirled it slightly to mix the substance in with the champagne.

Alarmed, Annalee glanced at Ewan whose attention was monopolized by Mr. McCauley.

When she looked back at the reflection of the waiter in the mirror, he was placing the glasses on a tray. It was easy to track the progress of the champagne that held the additional element, as the stem had a ring attached to the spot just above the base.

The waiter had just *poisoned* someone's drink!

And now he was carrying the tray and coming toward their table.

Her heart began to hammer hard inside her chest.

With fear climbing up her throat, she watched as the gentleman passed out the glasses and set the poisoned one in front of her. She stared at the bubbling, sparkling drink, and her palms began to sweat.

"Here we are," Mr. McCauley said. "Let's have a toast."

He was about to lift his glass, when Annalee blurted, "I'm so sorry."

The men paused and looked at her, waiting for her to finish her thought.

What to say? What to do?

She gulped. "I…I've suddenly remembered something and…and I need to speak to Ewan."

"It can't wait?" Mr. McCauley asked, his brow furrowing in consternation.

"No, I apologize. It's a f-feminine issue. Please forgive me. We'll be just a moment." She rose to her feet.

Ewan hopped up, his expression showing worry and some hesitancy.

A feminine issue? She mentally shook her head at herself, but it was the only thing that would allow her not to have to elaborate.

She walked away from the table, but only went so far as the center of the room. She needed to keep her eye on the glass. She turned to face Ewan, and he almost bumped into her.

"Sorry," he said hastily, his eyes wide with concern. "What's wrong?"

Using her peripheral vision, she kept tabs on the flute containing the poison. "Don't turn around. Don't move. Keep your posture as loose as you possibly can."

His dark brows furrowed. "All right."

She quickly relayed what she'd seen in the mirror, and it sounded so fantastical to her ears she began to doubt her vision. "Am I being ridiculous?" she couldn't help asking.

"No," Ewan ground out, his tone hard. Rage fired in his eyes. "There's been rumors about him being behind the deaths of other people."

"Oh, my God," she rasped.

Ewan cupped her elbow. "We need someone to go for the law, and we'll need to keep him from getting rid of the poisoned champagne. Can you still see it?"

She nodded slowly. "It hasn't moved, but he's staring us down."

"It's possible he's catching on that you've figured out the waiter laced your drink."

"What do you suppose is in there?"

"Easiest guess is arsenic." Ewan signaled the host of the restaurant.

The gentleman came over. "What is it? Is something wrong with your lady?"

"Yes. Please send someone for the Marshal. We have reason to believe there's been an attempt on her life."

Snapping to attention, the host said, "What's happened? What's going on?"

"Just fetch the law. This can all be handled discreetly, I promise," Ewan told him.

The man jerked a nod, then spun on a heel.

Ewan looked at Annalee, his expression determined. "Are you prepared to keep him at bay while we wait for the law?"

With Ewan at her side, she could do anything. "Yes," she replied firmly.

His mouth quirked up at the corners. "Good. Then let's go."

"Wait, we need a plan. He's going to want to go right back into the toast."

"Damn," Ewan said in low tones, "you're right."

She wracked her brain for a reason not to consume the champagne and only one thing came to mind. "I...I could pretend I'm pregnant."

Ewan stilled. "What now?"

She warmed to the idea, knowing she could pull this off. "Yes, I can tell him I'm two months along, and that alcohol makes me sick."

"All right," he drawled slowly, "but who's the father?"

And in the midst of the scariness, she found a moment of levity. She gave him a tiny grin. "Why, you, of course."

His eyes popped wide. "Uh, uh, I—"

She patted his upper arm and gave a light chuckle. "Just play along, I can do this." And with that she went back to their table with a smile for their villainous companion. "My apologies, Mr. McCauley. I had to do a lot of explaining."

A dubious light shone in the man's eyes as he replied, "That's not a problem. I hope you're to rights now."

As she resumed her seat, so did Ewan who thankfully had seemed to find his composure. "Not quite, but my trouble can certainly be avoided."

"Glad to hear it," Mr. McCauley said. He reached for his glass. "Now then—"

She held up a staying hand. "I going to have to remove myself from consuming any alcohol."

Annoyance flashed in his gaze. "Why?" he fairly barked.

She formed a secret, shy expression. "I'm two months along, Mr. McCauley."

The man narrowed his eyes. "Oh?"

She nodded. "And unfortunately, there are foods and drinks that make me sick, so I can't join in. I'd forgotten until just now and needed Ewan's permission to explain things to you."

Mr. McCauley slid a suspicious glance at Ewan. "What do you need his go-ahead for?"

Ewan crossed his arms over his chest. "Because I'm the father, and we're gettin' hitched when we get to Fort Worth."

His firm tone stunned Annalee to her core, and her pulse began to race.

"Well, that's—" Mr. McCauley's response was cut short when something behind Annalee caught his attention. The color drained from his cheeks, then he shot to his feet, "Sons-a-bitches!" He went for the gun in his coat pocket.

Annalee gasped as Ewan lunged at him. He plowed his shoulder into McCauley's gut. They crashed to the ground. Snarls from the fighting men and shouts from the other diners resounded through the room.

Panic ripped through Annalee, and she scrambled from her chair.

Ewan smashed a fist into McCauley's face.

A policeman raced past her, charging toward the grappling pair.

The host followed, but the bartender bearing down on her with fear in his eyes sent terror shooting up her spine. He was coming for the poisoned champagne!

She plucked it up and pedaled backward with it.

"Give that to me!" he roared.

With her heart thundering in her ears, she darted to the side, keeping the table between them.

Suddenly, their waiter tackled the bartender, pinning him to the ground.

She whipped her head toward Ewan and found him being held back by the host while the policeman had control of McCauley.

Suddenly, a shot blasted through the air.

Annalee hunkered down as screams echoed in the restaurant.

"All y'all quit your fightin' and your snarlin'!" a voice boomed. "What the hell is goin' on?"

The owner of the tone of authority strode forward, and it was easy to see the badge pinned to the black vest covering his broad chest. Once the Marshal had gone past her to where Ewan and McCauley were being held, Annalee rose slowly, her grip not faltering on the glass she still held.

She glanced toward the waiter and bartender and found the latter was knocked out cold. The waiter stood over him, a thunderous scowl on his face.

Ewan's angry, but unshakeable voice reached her as he succinctly explained what had happened.

McCauley broke in at various points, arguing his innocence.

"Where's the woman?" the Marshal demanded.

Eyes swiveled to her, and the Marshal spun around. He studied her for a moment, then pointed at the champagne she held. "That's the poisoned liquor?"

"Yes, sir." She heard the tremble in her voice. She looked at Ewan, and his gaze was sharp with determination and hot with anger.

The Marshal scanned the room. "Where's the bartender?"

The waiter raised his hand. "Here. I got him good, and he's out."

"Pick him up. Cart him to my office. Kirk, you go with him."

The officer did as his boss asked, while the Marshal himself strode to McCauley and grabbed him by the collar. "I'll take you. Where's his gun?"

Ewan's attention left her, and he stepped forward, raising his arm. "Here. I got it from him after I tackled him."

"Good man. Good man." The Marshal took it and shoved it into his waist band. "You and you," he pointed at Ewan and Annalee, "bring that glass to the office now." He yanked McCauley forward. "Let's go and don't you give me no trouble."

McCauley cussed and glared at Annalee as he was brought forward.

She stepped away, cautious and worried he might lunge for her. She butted up against a hard body and turned to see Ewan right behind her.

With the same penetrating, direct stare, his gaze roved over her face, and he cupped her cheek. "Are you all right?"

Her heart was quaking. Her knees were trembling, but she was not harmed. "Yes."

He watched her for a few silent moments, then carefully, gently, took the glass from her. "Come on."

And she plastered herself close to his side as they left the restaurant.

Chapter Six

Slashes of moonlight coming through the windows flanking her bed painted her room in a silver glow. But the sharp shadows of the unfamiliar space tormented her. Those dark spots snared her focus and robbed her of rest. Anything could be lurking. Threats could rain down. Pain could come in an instant, catching her unaware.

With her pulse pounding hard, she sat up in bed. Her balance had been shaken. Her peace had been taken. Evil lived in this world, and she'd witnessed it tonight, had almost been its victim.

She'd been lucky. *Ewan* had been lucky. By his enraged strength and sheer will, he'd kept Buck McCauley from letting off even one shot.

If she hadn't seen the waiter put the arsenic in her champagne, she would be dead right now. And all because of someone's greed.

She wasn't going to be able to rest.

She got up and began to pace, her linen nightgown fluttering softly against her legs. She relived every second of the evening, her mind unable to completely grasp the reality.

They'd been escorted into the Marshal's office when they'd arrived at the police station, and the glass had been whisked away from them. After a half-hour of waiting, the Marshal had appeared, and Ewan and Annalee had been informed that the bartender had regained consciousness in his cell. The man had confessed to his part in order to escape a stiffer punishment.

The law had used the Marsh test to determine if the drink had been laced. And the results had been positive. She recalled the rush of dizziness that had assailed her at the news, and again she'd been immensely thankful for Ewan's solid presence next to her.

He was a calming, helpful force, and she was growing used to the regularity of it. When she'd started this journey, she'd assumed it would be a frustrating experience. And it still was, but for an all together different reason.

She loved a man who did not love her.

She stopped her anxious trek and gazed longingly at the connecting door. She *missed* him. Her heart yearned and ached for his comfort.

An attempt had been made on her life. And she was in a room, alone. She was *alone.*

But Ewan's statement outside of Finch's Feed rushed back with astounding strength. He'd told her then, in soft but strong tones, that she was *not* alone. He had implied that she could lean on him. Depend on him.

She took in a deep breath as her feet propelled her closer to the door. What was she doing? Oh, she couldn't seek him out! She *shouldn't*!

And yet she continued on.

As she came around the bed, she saw a soft glow of light peeking beneath the bottom of the door.

Encouraged by the sight, she discarded her mental protestations, and quickened her pace. She didn't pause as she rapped lightly.

A rustling came from within, and not even a second later, the knob was turned and the door yanked open.

He stood there, his dark hair falling over his forehead, his shirt unbuttoned. He looked as unsettled as she felt.

"I..." She gulped. "I can't sleep."

Without a word, he took her in hand, pushed farther into her room, shut the door with his foot, then pulled her into his arms.

His embrace was as solid as steel, but as warm as a summer's day. She melted, leaning into him, and allowed any walls she had to crumble. She needed this. She needed *him*.

He rested his chin on the top of her head.

The strong, steady beat of his heart comforted her as much as his hold. And he'd taken her into his arms without even a word. Not even a protest. As if he needed her close just as much.

She swallowed and moved her arms from between their bodies and wrapped them around his waist.

He let out a breath.

They stayed that way for several minutes, and she realized that even though he might not love her, he did care. Which was good. Not good enough, but still...good.

When the clock in her room struck fifteen minutes after midnight, she gently stepped out of his embrace. She wanted to stay there, and it hurt to move away, but she couldn't take advantage. Besides, she didn't want him to know the depth of her feelings. "Thank you," she said softly. "I needed that."

He said nothing. Just slipped his hands into the pockets of his denims.

She took in a deep breath then let it out. "I'm so...unsettled over what happened and what could've happened."

He nodded once.

"The world is ugly right now, and I can't seem to get past it."

The moonlight illuminated his strong features, and his jaw worked with the need to speak. But, in the end, he said nothing.

She understood. What was there to say?

Suddenly, his deep voice broke through. "I won't let anything happen to you."

His promise comforted and concerned her. "I'm so thankful that you want to protect me, but I worry for your safety, as well. You could've died tonight, too." Her heart ripped as her imagination conjured blood staining his chest. "I...please...don't put yourself in harm's way for me."

The lines of his face tightened with anger. "I'll do what's necessary. I'm not gonna let anyone hurt you. Never again."

She was surprised by the strength of his conviction. "You won't be with me every second."

He didn't immediately respond, and his expression went harsh with pain as if her point had cut him to the bone. "I'll figure something out," he argued, his tone hard with promise. "Maybe you should hire security."

And suddenly her fear was snuffed out and replaced by alarm. "Oh, surely not. Surely..." She shook her head. "We're overreacting. We have to be. We shouldn't make decisions like this when barely six hours have passed since the...trouble."

He pressed his lips into a thin line, then rubbed the back of his neck as he thought about her words.

"Do you have suspicions that other cattle barons will come after me like that?"

As he shook his head, he lowered his arm. "No. But you'll get more offers. And every ranch needs to watch for signs of sabotage and water grabbing."

Worried, she licked her bottom lip as possible problems ran through her mind. "It's a dangerous business, but...you and the other cowboys have so much experience. I trust y'all with everything."

Ewan's mouth quirked up in a distracted smile. He still seemed concerned.

Because he didn't feel he could trust her as she trusted him? Tumult churned in her stomach. She knew she would have to prove herself, just as he and the other hands had had to prove themselves to her father. It was all part of the process, and she'd learned from the best. She reached out and cupped his upper arm. "Please don't worry. I can handle this job. I can—"

"I know," he ground out. "I watched that...*bastard* interrogate you, and you didn't break once. You were much calmer than I was. I would've told him to go to hell, but you acted just like your father would've."

Surprised, she tightened her fingers around his muscular bicep. "You think so?"

"I know so. And you recognized quickly that your drink had been poisoned, and you handled telling me in such a way that bought us a fair amount of time."

She hadn't expected his praise. Undone, she rasped, "Thank you, Ewan. I appreciate hearing that."

His face softened, and his posture loosened. "You thought fast. Came up with a pretty good tale."

She remembered his shock when she suggested he was the father of her pretend baby, and she chuckled. "We're lucky you didn't faint when I gave you your role."

He grinned. "Didn't expect you to say I was the father, even if it was fake."

She realized she was still touching him and lowered her arm, covering the too-long contact with, "Well, we *have* been getting along better, haven't we?"

"Seems as if we are. You're not mad at me all the time, like usual."

"And you aren't teasing me as much, *like usual*."

He didn't reply, but his grin was still affixed.

Silence fell between them, and she grew aware that she was alone with him, in her bedroom, with only her nightgown on. This was highly inappropriate, but...she didn't want him to leave.

Her skin began to tingle, and it took all of her will not to glance down at his chest revealed by his unbuttoned shirt.

He cleared his throat nervously, as if he was also noticing the intimacy of the setting. "Are you gonna be all right?"

If she said yes, he would leave. If she said no...

"I…I don't…" She couldn't find the courage to go forward with the outcome of either answer.

He shifted from foot to foot. "I can stay a little longer." He gazed at her with a concerned expression. "If you want."

She swallowed hard, temptation battling inside her. "You…You wouldn't mind?"

He cleared his throat again. "No."

She gestured at the padded bench resting against the footboard. "We could sit."

"Sure."

They moved together and lowered to the cushion. Silence fell between them.

As they sat in the moonlit darkness, awkwardness grew. She slipped her hands beneath her thighs and wracked her brain for anything to talk about. But his nearness clouded her thoughts, and all she could do was imagine him taking her in his arms again.

The emotions swirling inside her were tiring, and despite her agitation, she had to stifle a yawn.

"Here," he said softly, scooting closer and lifting his arm. "Lean on me, and maybe you'll go to sleep."

Oh! How wonderful. How sweet. How…

She melted and moved into him, resting her head against his chest while he held her gently. This had to be what being in Heaven would feel like.

As her heart thumped wildly, she soaked up his presence, his strength, and her spirit calmed. Soon, her eyes closed, and she slept.

ANNALEE JERKED AWAKE, and she blinked at the ceiling, trying to get her mind working. She recalled the evening before, the ugliness…

Then the sweetness of…

Ewan!

She bolted upright, searching for him.

When she saw him sleeping in the chair in the corner, relief poured through her. She slumped and placed a palm to her pounding heart. He hadn't left.

But sometime in the night, he'd carried her to bed. A vision of him taking care of her so sweetly formed in her mind and made her heart squeeze with longing and love. How she wished he loved her back, and how she hoped he didn't take the offer he had from Beau Wilton of the Double Bar.

As she nibbled on her lip, she checked the clock on the side table. It was seven in the morning. They probably needed to get up and get going.

She climbed out of bed and padded over to him, enjoying the sight of him relaxed in sleep. She paused an arm's length from him, loath to wake him.

He looked so peaceful and boyish. He was so wonderful. Her heart melted as she studied him, and dangerous thoughts of confessing her feelings began to race through her mind. She fiddled with her fingers, fearful but helpless to what she wanted.

What would be the harm in telling him what he meant to her?

He flinched in his sleep, and alarm shot up her spine. Hastily, she reached out and lightly shook his shoulder.

As he came awake, she took a step back, her heart in her throat that he could've caught her watching him. Perhaps it *wouldn't* be a good idea to tell him that she loved him.

He rubbed his face, then blinked a couple times before focusing on her. "Oh. Morning. Sorry."

She shook her head, fearful to speak because of what she might say.

He pushed to his feet. "I didn't want to leave you in case you woke up and got scared again."

He was too wonderful. She couldn't stand it. "Thank you," she rasped.

With a narrowing of his eyes at the morning sun coming through the windows, he asked, "What is it? Seven?"

"Yes."

He yawned then scratched the back of his neck. "Guess we ought to get going."

She made no reply as her heart rebelled against them leaving this room. She would remember this night for a long time. Perhaps for forever. "I...I suppose we should."

His brow furrowed. "Are you all right?"

"Yes," she rasped, then shook out of her lovesickness, "yes. Just waking up."

"Not thinking about last night at all?" he asked gently.

She shook her head slowly, wishing she could tell him that he had obliterated all her fears.

"Good." He gave a quick smile. "See you in the lobby in an hour?"

"Sure."

With that, he went around her toward the connecting door. She heard it open and shut, and sadness gripped her. He was gone.

THEY DIDN'T STAY LONG in Waco. They stopped only to retrieve the letter and confirm that Fort Worth was the last stop. They were instructed to pick up the last communication at the Stagecoach Inn.

When they reached the bustling city of Fort Worth, Annalee's eyes went wide. As they rode through the town toward the inn, she took in as much as she could. It was a cow town, that was for sure. Austin was for the politician. Fort Worth was made for the cowboy.

Saloons, auctions, rodeos, gambling halls, and dance halls lined the streets. The stockyards were a bevy of commerce.

They stopped at a rodeo and watched from outside the arena. The trick riding and roping amazed her, and she was also astounded by some of the performers' saddles. The stitching and scrollwork was beautiful and intricate.

After leaving the show, they trotted on toward the inn, and she delighted in many of the shops on the way. She turned to Ewan who's sharp gaze was on the road ahead. "I'd love to go shopping once we get settled."

He turned toward her and gave her a soft, indulgent smile. "All right."

"I could buy something for Delly."

His gaze glinted with fondness. "That'd be real nice of you."

Excited, she grinned back at him. "Fort Worth is an interesting town."

He chuckled, then looked ahead. "Yeah, the fellas always enjoyed coming, but we'll steer clear of where the main action is."

"Oh?" Curious, she leaned toward him. "There's an even livelier section of town?"

He shook his head. "We're not going there. It's one of the most dangerous places in Texas."

She straightened, shocked. "In *Texas*?"

He nodded.

"And our friends spent time there?"

"Sure did."

She pressed her lips into a thin line, imagining all sorts of horrors. Probably shoot outs. Probably dangerous card games. And...women. Probably.

Alarm gripped her as a thought occurred, and she gripped Epona's reins more tightly. "Did my father go there?"

"To Hell's Half Acre?" Ewan grunted and shook his head hard. "Hell no."

Her breath whooshed out of her. Thank goodness. She didn't want to wonder if her father had partaken in the vice that such a place probably held.

Of course...*Ewan* could've reveled in the various...activities.

She began to nibble on her lower lip, worried that he might enjoy those sorts of...things. Perhaps that was one of the reasons why he didn't seem to have any interest in her. Perhaps she wasn't the type of woman he...usually liked.

"No more questions?" he asked as they came to a busy intersection.

She had several, but she wasn't going to voice them. He might reveal something that would break her heart. She cleared her throat. "I think the name of the place is terrifying enough. I don't need to know more."

He chuckled low. "Don't worry. I won't take you within a mile of that part of town."

How she wished his dedication to her safety and protection meant that he cared for her. She swallowed a lump of sorrow and sadness.

They arrived at the inn, then tied their horses and the mule to the hitching post. The Stagecoach Inn was a wooden structure that appeared to have seen better days, but Annalee recalled it was the rooming house her parents had stayed in after they'd gotten married in the spring of '77.

When they entered, a stooped gentleman, with snow white hair, and a tan, weathered face rose from his chair behind a small desk.

Annalee smiled, realizing she was about to meet Chester Albertson, the man who'd fetched the priest for her parents. "Hello, Mr. Albertson," she said happily when she reached the desk.

The man smiled. "And you're Green Eyes, ain't ya?"

"Yes, sir."

"Knew it. Knew it as soon as ya come in. You're the spittin' image of your mama, and God bless but your papa was right about those eyes of yours."

Her heart swelled with love for her parents. "I'm so pleased to meet you." She gestured toward Ewan who stood behind and to the right of her. "This is my foreman, Ewan Judge."

Mr. Albertson inclined his head. "I've heard the name. Seems some folks find you as the best cowboy in the state, son."

Ewan slipped his hands into his pockets. "I'm not sure about that. Just do my job."

"And that's what the Lord asks of us, ain't it? That's all we gotta do. All for His glory."

Annalee was charmed by this older, weathered, wise gentleman. "Yes, sir."

He cleared his throat and changed the subject. "I suspect you're here for your letters."

Surprised, Annalee questioned, "Letters? There's more than one?"

Turning toward a set of boxes inset into the wall, he said, "Yep. Three, in fact. Got one for Miss Gillespie and two for Mr. Judge."

She shared a look with Ewan who wore a surprised expression himself.

He shrugged, then stepped slightly forward to retrieve his mail.

The envelopes were passed out.

"One to you from your papa, Miss Gillespie. One to Judge from Jack, as well, and then another to Judge from a Mr. Wilton of the Double Bar."

Annalee almost crumpled the envelope in a tight fist at the name of the sender for Ewan's second letter.

Mr. Wilton of the Double Bar.

He was the cattle baron who'd offered Ewan a job.

Her throat went dry with aching sadness and immense anxiety. She didn't want to raise steers without Ewan. She didn't want to do *life* without Ewan.

Before she could let tears take over, she turned away and opened her letter. She could hear Ewan doing the same.

She set her focus on her father's words and tried not to think about what Ewan was reading.

Miss Green Eyes,

Here you are at the final stop before the Red River crossing. Not much to see there anymore, so there's no reason for y'all to go any farther. Besides, I'm hopeful you'll spend a few days here and enjoy the cow town. You might meet some of your fellow cattle barons if you do.

I'm proud of you, Annalee. The situation you're in can't be easy. After your mother died, I wanted to be prepared and to teach you as much as I could in case something happened to me.

And something did happen to me if you're reading this. I'm real sorry about that. Even now, as I write this, I feel grief and sorrow for what you're going through.

I don't ever want to leave you alone. I'll do my best not to for as long as I can. But if I pass on, you gotta know, everyone at the Circle G loves you. They'll care for you, and they'll help you.

Sweet girl, you've always been the light of my eye. I told your mama on the day you were born that I couldn't fathom why our Lord would let me be your papa. There's something about a daughter that makes a man realize just how blessed he is. That the Lord entrusted me with you astounds me and makes me wonder what He's thinking. But I wouldn't give you up for the world.

I know I said there would be a surprise for you at the end of this, and I hope it works out. If it does, know that I'm thrilled and smiling down on you. If it doesn't, well, it won't be your fault.

Have a good life, Green Eyes. Always know that me, your mama, and Ramsey love you.

Papa

A deluge of sobs and tears threatened, and she dashed out of the inn. She heard Ewan call her name, but she didn't turn around. She hurried down the walk, taking deep breaths and trying to control her emotions.

She swiped at the tears that managed to escape, dodging people as she kept a brisk pace. She had no idea where she was going, but she had had to get out. Get away.

Her family was gone. She would never see them again. Grief stormed through her as her future promised nothing more than bleakness.

She wasn't alone, no, but...

She *was*. She *was* on her own. She didn't have a family. She didn't have a partner.

With trembling fingers, she shoved her father's letter into her skirt pocket. Where was she going? She scanned her surroundings, looking for a place that would provide her with some privacy.

A church steeple rose over the buildings lining the busy street, and she quickened her steps. As she crossed the road, she was careful around the wagons that rumbled over the dirt lane. She raced up onto the boardwalk, anxious to be within the walls of the church.

Just as she came abreast of an alleyway, strong, biting fingers wrapped around her left shoulder and an arm clamped around her waist. She turned to see who had her, but she was shoved into the alley.

She stumbled and fell, the heel of her hand scraping on the rocks, and her hip slamming onto the hard, unforgiving ground. Pain sliced through her, and she cried out.

A punishing grip on her arm yanked her to standing.

Before she could get out a scream, she was shoved against the wall, and she cracked her skull. Her vision blurred, and her breath left her.

The body of her attacker pressed mercilessly against her, and a menacing voice hissed, "You ruined my life. I'm gonna ruin yours."

Her attacker's face came into focus, and terror shot through her. McCauley!

She bucked against him and screamed, but he put a meaty hand over her mouth, muffling the sound.

Rage coursed through her. Righteous fury consumed her, and she exploded. She bit the hand that covered her mouth, and as he howled in pain, she brought up her leg and kneed him in the groin.

He doubled over, his grip on her easing up.

She wrenched away from him, snatched up an empty crate lying in the alley, brought it over her head then smashed it across his back.

He wobbled but didn't fall.

With her heart roaring in her ears, she picked up a brick and hit the side of his face.

The force spun him, and his body flailed into the brick wall of one of the shops.

But still, he did not go down.

She dashed toward the entrance to the street, but he tackled her, slamming her to the ground. Gravel sliced into her chest and arms, and she bit the inside of her cheek.

Suddenly, his weight was lifted off her.

Snarls resounded, and the sound of bone striking flesh reached her.

On trembling arms, she pushed to stand and found Ewan pummeling her attacker. "Ewan!" she cried, relieved but terrified of the hate and rage behind his punches.

Whistles shrilled through the air, and she spun toward the noise. Men in police uniforms barreled toward her, and she plastered herself to the wall of one of the shops as they raced by her.

They had hold of both men before she could get a word out.

"Don't hurt, Ewan!" she cried, dashing forward. "He was saving me! Don't arrest him! Please!"

But Ewan battled against the men that held him, trying to get to McCauley who fought consciousness and hung limply in the hold of two policemen.

The officers slammed Ewan to the ground and cuffed him.

"No!" she cried, her heart breaking. "He didn't do anything!"

As Ewan was hauled to his feet, one of the men holding McCauley barked, "Ma'am!"

She spun in his direction.

With his dark brows drawn in a thunderous expression, he commanded, "Follow us to the station unless you're hurt. We'll get someone to take you to the hospital if you are."

She wasn't leaving Ewan for anything. "I'm fine. But Ewan didn't do anything."

The men said nothing and began walking their prisoners out of the alley.

Annalee clamped her mouth shut, though anger coursed through her. She met Ewan's stare as they dragged him past her.

The intense need to get to her shone bright in his brown eyes. He even fought the hands that held him for a moment, but the policemen tightened their grip and one warned, "Don't make it worse."

Without a word, Annalee strode after them, ignoring the onlookers and the pain from the wounds she felt along her chest and arms and in her cheek. They were going to let Ewan go...or suffer her wrath.

Chapter Seven

Annalee paced the Marshal's office, fuming. They'd taken Ewan into the bowels of the station despite her protests.

The door opened, and a gentleman in a three piece suit walked in. "Miss Gillespie?"

"Where's Ewan?"

The lanky man smiled, his hazel eyes shining with a kind light. "My name is Steven Spencer. I'm the District Attorney."

"Wonderful. Where's Ewan?"

"Would you like to sit—"

"No, I wouldn't, and I demand an answer *now*." She curled her hands into fists, ignoring the pain from the scrapes she'd received when trying to catch herself from falling during the attack.

The lawyer held his hands up, palms out. "He's fine. He's giving his account to the Marshal, and I've come to get yours." He gestured at a green leather chair. "Please. Make yourself comfortable."

She gritted her teeth, then twitched her lips, thinking. If she did as he asked, would she get to see Ewan more quickly? The possibility encouraged her. "Fine. But let's make this quick. I thought this problem was completed in Austin. I can't tell you how frightened I was to see Buck McCauley only a few days after he tried to kill me the first time." She lowered to the seat.

Mr. Spencer leaned against the edge of the Marshal's desk and folded his arms over his chest. "He tried to kill you earlier?"

With a calm she didn't feel, Annalee succinctly went through the events that had occurred in Austin.

Mr. Spencer listened with an intent expression and appeared to miss nothing.

"I suppose Mr. McCauley escaped," she surmised, "and then came after me. He knew my father was sending Ewan and me on a trip up the Chisolm, and that made it easy for him to find me. When he attacked me, he told me that since I'd ruined his life, he was going to ruin mine." The memory of his evil voice made her quake inside, but she *refused* to tremble on the outside.

Mr. Spencer rubbed his chin. "Even though he'd escaped, he couldn't go back to his life." He lowered his arm and shook his head. "I despise criminals." He pushed to his feet. "Miss Gillespie, I humbly apologize for what you've been through. We'll keep McCauley under lock and key better than the men down in Austin, I can promise you that."

She rose. "I would like to see Ewan."

He nodded. "Of course. I believe he was coming to your aid, and" Mr. Spencer smiled, "by the way he demanded to see you I could tell you are his primary concern."

Yes, her safety was important to him. Her father had charged him with the job, and Ewan was going to take it seriously. "He's my foreman."

Mr. Spencer arched an eyebrow. "Seems like he's more than that."

She clammed up, dismayed that this stranger had quickly and easily read her feelings.

He waved a hand. "I beg your pardon. It's none of my business." He moved toward the door. "I'll fetch him for you. He should be done."

After he left, she sat back down, upset and anxious. Things were all jumbled up...her emotions...their journey...Ewan's possible departure from the Circle G.

While they'd gotten along and had even formed a surprising friendship, there'd still been so much trouble. She was probably more of a problem than he wanted to handle.

Because McCauley might not be her only enemy. Ewan had said that sabotage was common among competing cattle barons. And her father had eventually explained that range wars were possible. She would hate to be a distraction to Ewan while in the middle of a fight, especially since he could be injured or worse.

According to many, he was the best cowboy in the state, and he should be using his talents to their fullest extent. Perhaps she should give him permission to go. Maybe he was struggling to take Mr. Wilton's offer because of his loyalty to her family.

The door burst open, and she shot to her feet and spun.

Ewan was already to her, and he cupped her upper arms, assessing her with an earnest expression. "Are you all right? Are you hurt?"

"I...n-not really. Just a few scrapes and bruises."

His gaze leapt with fiery rage. "That *bastard*," he growled. "I should've killed him!"

"Oh, Ewan, no," she rasped, knives slicing her heart at what she was going to have to do. "Please, don't be upset. I'm all right." She forced a smile. "I smashed a crate over him and hit him with a brick, too."

Ewan's brow lifted, but his face was still tight with anger. "Good, but you *never* should've had to do it. How in the *hell* did he escape the jail in Austin?"

She didn't know and it didn't matter. Gently, she extracted herself from his hold. "It's just been so...unbelievable. All this...trouble."

With a shaky hand, he rubbed his forehead. "I know. I'm sorry. I couldn't find you for several minutes, but it felt like forever. And—"

She held up a staying hand, interrupting him. "Don't. No. Please."

He lowered his arm and frowned at her. "Don't what?"

"Scold yourself. None of what happened is your fault."

His frown deepened. "Annalee—"

"Come, let's sit." Her heart pounded hard as the knives she'd willingly inserted into it cut more deeply. She took one of the leather chairs.

With an uncertain, unsettled expression, he took the seat beside her, then waited.

How to start? What to say? She had to make sure he understood how much she valued him. Her throat went dry, and tears pricked, but she blinked them away. She had to do what was right for the man she loved.

"When we started this journey," she began, "I wasn't happy. You and I have had an adversarial relationship for many years." She gave a rueful chuckle. "But things have changed, and there's *no* praise, *no* compliments, no...*accolades* good enough to describe you, Ewan Judge."

His cheeks went ruddy, and he shifted. "Thanks."

"I'm glad we were able to spend this time together, and" she splayed a hand over her chest, "I'm...*beyond* grateful that you put yourself in danger for me."

"Annalee—"

"Please let me finish." She had to get it out or she might not ever say it.

He pressed his lips together, acquiescing.

"I...I don't think it's fair to you, with all your talents, to spend your years with an inexperienced person as your boss. Not to mention one that would need saving." She swallowed.

He went still.

Strain rose between them.

She linked her fingers together tightly, frustrated with herself that she might've upset him. "I know you have a job offer from the Double Bar."

His eyes widened a fraction.

The lump of sorrow sitting at the base of her throat increased in size. Breathing became difficult. "If you feel that what Mr. Wilton has offered is better, I want you to be free to take it. Please don't stay with me out of loyalty to my father. You deserve to have the best position possible. You're a good man, well-respected, and knowledgeable. If the

Circle G isn't a place that will allow you to achieve whatever you desire, then you...you m-must go."

That was all she could say. The pain slicing through her made it impossible to speak any longer. Her grip on her fingers had turned punishing, and she held herself rigidly as she waited for him to respond.

An agonizing second passed by.

Then another.

He opened his mouth but looked stunned. Uncertain. He said nothing.

What had she done? Had she hurt him?

The door opened, and Marshal York walked in. "Well, folks. You're free to go. Got McCauley behind bars, and Austin's sendin' someone up this way to help determine where he ought to be tried now." His round face sported a wide grin, and the sunlight streaming in through the windows made his bald head shine.

Annalee shot to her feet. "Thank you so much. I would like to rest and tend to the few scrapes I have."

Marshal York's blond brows knitted. "The boys told me you weren't hurt."

She waved a hand. "They asked if I needed to go to the hospital, and I said it wasn't necessary. I can take care of my injuries myself."

"Ma'am—"

"I'm fine, Marshal York," she said, moving to the door. "I'll just head back to the inn now, since we're done." She needed to escape Ewan and the conversation they'd had. Without looking back, she left the room and hurried down the corridor toward the main entrance.

Rapid steps sounded behind her, then a familiar grip latched onto her elbow.

She briefly closed her eyes. "Ewan, I—"

"Let's not," he practically growled.

She closed her mouth and let him escort her to the Stagecoach Inn.

His firm hold on her made her heart race, and her insides quake. She longed for him, and at the same time, wanted to flee from whatever anger or hurt she'd caused him. She chewed on her bottom lip as he hurried her down the walk.

They dodged others who were out taking care of whatever business they had, going past the shops that Annalee had wanted to patronize only a couple of hours before. How she wished she felt the ease from earlier that would allow her to enjoy this cow town.

This was their last stop. The quest her father had sent her on was over, and she'd completed the tasks he'd set for her. Suddenly, she remembered the prize they were supposed to have been given.

They reached the inn, and Ewan let go of her once they were in the lobby. As he stepped up to the desk, encountering Mr. Albertson's questioning gaze, she removed her father's letter from her skirt pocket.

While Ewan spoke with Mr. Albertson, she scanned the final communication, finding the sentences she was looking for.

I know I said there would be a surprise for you at the end of this, and I hope it works out. If it does, know that I'm thrilled and smiling down on you. If it doesn't, well, it won't be your fault.

Not her fault? He hoped it worked out?

What could he mean?

Confused, she refolded the letter. Maybe Ewan would know to what her father referred. Hadn't Ewan received a letter also? Maybe he had more of an explanation.

"Here," Ewan said, handing her they key to the room he'd secured for her. "Albertson took care of everything. Our horses are at the livery and our bags are in our rooms."

The tight set of Ewan's jaw caused rocks to form in her stomach. He was upset with her. He was hurting. With trembling fingers, she took the key. "Th-Thank you."

"We've got a few hours before supper," he said gruffly. "You would probably like to rest."

"Y-Yes, that would be welcome." What could she say to smooth things over? She had to make sure he understood that she didn't want him go. She just wanted what was best for him.

When he took her elbow once more and began to walk her to a corridor to the left of the desk, she wracked her brain for the right words. None were coming. Her nerves were too frazzled for her mind to form anything logical or coherent. But her heart was too engaged to allow him to believe she didn't care so she spoke anyway.

"Ewan, about what I said earlier, I don't mean to upset you or hurt you. You mean the world to my family and to the Circle G. Of course, I don't want to lose you, but I couldn't bear it if I held you back from a better future."

He stopped in front of the door she assumed was hers.

She wasn't ready to leave him. She hadn't said enough. "We've become friends now, haven't we? We've learned to get along, and—" She stopped her babbling as a thought struck. "Oh! The surprise." She smiled tentatively. "Ewan, I know why Papa sent us on this trip."

"Do you?" he questioned, his tone gravelly and hard.

"Yes. Don't you see? We're friends now. At least, I see us as such. Papa made us go up the Chisolm together, so we'd learn more about each other and, hopefully, repair our relationship." She smiled wider. "And we did, didn't we?"

A muscle ticked in Ewan's tight jaw.

Disquiet snatched away the pleasure at her revelation. "Aren't we friends?" she asked hesitantly.

He glanced away, giving her his profile.

Her stomach dropped to her toes, and her heart broke. "Ewan, I...I'm so sorry. I—"

"Stop talking," he suddenly growled, his gaze whipping to hers. "Just stop."

She clamped her mouth shut. She'd read things incorrectly. She'd stepped into his world and had thought she'd known what she was doing. She hadn't.

Ewan Judge had always been a mystery to her, and he still was.

"I'll pick you up in three hours for supper," he told her roughly, then he walked away.

SHE'D HAD A BATH AND had taken care of the scrapes on her hands. The bruises along her ribs and hip weren't too bad and should fade after a couple of weeks.

It was an hour before six. Soon, Ewan would be knocking on her door.

As she'd taken care of herself, she'd mentally shoved away their very one-sided conversation, and his very abrupt and gruff reaction. Now, with nothing to do, it was coming back to her.

To distract herself, she retrieved a notebook from her bag and began making a list of what she wanted to accomplish when she arrived home. She included doing her own research on cross-breeding. She also jotted a note to speak to the foreman of the Split Hairs outfit. Mr. McCauley would more than likely be stripped of his assets, which would include the spread he'd most recently bought.

The man had no children, but perhaps he had had forethought and had constructed a will.

Even if he had, it would be to the Circle G's benefit to inquire about the future of the Split Hairs. If she could merge her range with the outfit, it would only allow her to increase her stock.

A hard, loud pounding at her door made her yelp and flinch.

She checked the small ormolu clock on the desk where she was sitting. Only a quarter past. Was her visitor Ewan? If so, why was he early? Had something happened?

With her pulse skipping erratically, she cautiously walked on trembling knees toward the door. "Who is it?" she called.

"Ewan."

She let out a breath, relieved.

But...why was he early? To tell her he was going to take the offer from the Double Bar?

Anxious, she smoothed her palms over her black skirt. Her stomach swirled with apprehension, but she unlocked the door and opened it.

He pushed inside, looking more agitated than she had ever seen him. Immediately, he began to pace the small area in front of the bed.

Uncertain of what had him upset, she slowly closed them inside. Had her words from before bothered him so much? Or perhaps she'd been wrong about the information contained within Mr. Wilton's letter.

Her nerves kept her silent. She had no idea what was wrong but wasn't going to guess any longer. She waited with her heart in her throat for him to say something.

He continued his pacing, his face drawn in tight, harsh lines.

The seconds ticked by.

The strain between them only thickened, and it took all of her willpower to remain quiet.

But he kept worriedly pacing, intermittently glancing at her.

What was wrong? What was going on? What—

Suddenly, he whipped to face her. "I love you. These days with you have been an agony I can't describe."

Her breath left her. Her heart stopped.

"I've loved you from the moment I saw you." His eyes were bright with feeling, with imploring. "You were the boss's daughter, though. And I have a hard time—" he broke off, as if it was too much for him to say. He let out a breath. "I love you, Annalee. So much. You've captivated me. You've…" his throat worked with emotion, "enthralled me. I don't ever want to be apart from you. I don't—"

He broke off, his gaze filled with harsh desperation as he looked at her. A muscle ticked at his jaw line.

Her mind couldn't catch hold of a thought. She felt dizzy. Blindly, she fumbled for the chair behind her, and she fell into the seat, her back to the mirrored vanity.

He cursed and shoved an angry hand through his hair. Then without warning stormed toward her. "Here," he said gruffly, abruptly, as he reached into the back pocket of his denims, "read this. It'll prove I'm telling the truth."

With disbelief stealing every faculty she owned, she took the envelope with trembling fingers.

He moved away from her as hastily as he'd come, then stood with his legs apart and his arms crossed. He shifted from foot to foot and wasn't looking at her.

She swallowed, trying to think through the impossibility of his words. But she was too struck, too faint. His declaration couldn't be true. It just *couldn't*.

But Ewan Judge was no liar.

And he'd handed her proof.

She gulped again and withdrew the letter. The date at the top, written in her father's hand, told her this was the letter Ewan had received today.

Ewan,

You got her here. Hopefully, you've fixed things. This is where her mother and I got married. St. Martin's is as fine a place as any, and she'll love it. Albertson'll help you fetch rings.

Ewan, son, if you haven't already done it, tell her how you feel. Now. Just get it out. It's been hell watching the two of you keep walls up between you, but it's all your fault. Not hers. You've got no one else but yourself to blame.

Get it done.

Jack

Her heart began to pound. She read the words a second time. A third. They didn't change.

Ewan loved her. And her father had known it. He'd even known that *Annalee* loved Ewan. He'd detected her walls.

Oh...

Tears formed, but she blinked them away.

Ewan loved her.

Ewan...*loved* her.

She jerked up her head and dropped the letter.

His face was turned away, anxious fear taking over every handsome, rugged line.

She flew toward him.

He lowered his arms as his brow lifted in surprise.

She launched herself at him.

He caught her with a whoosh of breath. As he held her tightly, he begged, "Tell me what this means. What—"

She pulled back and cupped his face, joy filling her soul. "You love me?"

His gaze shone with helplessness and pleading. "Yes."

Tears flooded her eyes. "Oh, Ewan." She exhaled slowly and any doubt, strain, or grief that remained fled from her. "I love you, too."

Awe came over his face. "Annalee," he breathed.

She couldn't believe what had happened. In an instant, things had changed. *Life* had changed. She gazed at him, undone, stunned.

The light in his eyes warmed. He lowered his head an inch.

She raised hers, lifting her face toward him, accepting his silent request.

He closed the remaining distance between their mouths, and she went up on her toes to meet him.

His lips fit to hers perfectly, and the feel of him sent tingles flying over her skin.

He deepened their kiss, using his tongue, and soon the contact became urgent, desperate.

She loved him! Oh, how she did! And he loved her!

He didn't want to be apart from her. He wanted *her*. *She* was enough.

Abruptly, he broke the kiss and dropped to one knee. With his hands still clutching her waist, and his gaze still filled with fiery longing, he asked, "Will you marry me?"

Her heart flew to the heavens. Oh, good gracious!

"Will you? Now? Before we leave this city? Maybe you need me to court you, and if you do, I won't argue. But I can't live much longer without you. The past years have been a torment."

The agony in his tone matched the feelings that had been coursing through her during all the time she'd known him. Waiting was not what she wanted. "I will marry you tonight if you can manage it."

Determination immediately took over his face, and he shot to his feet. "That's a yes, then."

She nodded.

"You're gonna be my wife."

"Yes." She reveled in how intently he was looking at her, how his body snapped with firm resolve. He would not be dissuaded now that she'd given her agreement.

"Meet me in the lobby at six."

She nodded.

He gave her a look, then strode to the door and left.

Chapter Eight

She changed into the pale pink, silk evening dress that she'd worn to the opera house in Beeville. She redid her bun, making her locks form more softly around her face.

He'd told her to meet him in the lobby at six, which gave him not much more than a half hour to prepare for a wedding. Had he managed to find rings?

But she honestly didn't care.

They were in love!

Ewan Judge, the man she'd loved for so long, loved her. How could this be? And he'd said he'd *always* loved her, that the past years had been a torment.

He had a lot of explaining to do she thought, as she smiled at her reflection in the mirror.

A knock came at her door.

With a lift of her brow and the tiniest bit of fear that he'd changed his mind, she moved toward the summons. "Who is it?"

"Chester Albertson."

Quickly, she turned the knob and opened the door. She smiled at the older man. "Good evening."

"Miss Gillespie," he replied with a slight bow and a twinkle in his eyes. "I've come to fetch you."

"Have you?"

"I'm takin' you to the church, just like I did your mama."

"Oh?" She hadn't known that. "I thought—"

"I'll tell you the story," he interrupted, crooking his elbow at her, "on the way."

Hastily, she shut the door and locked it, then eagerly accepted his escort. "I want every detail."

"Well," he began as he led her down the hall, "your papa got here first. Your mama was comin' on the train from Topeka, and your papa was chompin' at the bit, let me tell you. He paced these streets, *and* these halls for three days."

They reached the lobby, but Ewan was not in sight.

"As soon as your mama showed, that boy wanted to rush her off to the church. No freshening up. No rings. And he hadn't even told the priest." Mr. Albertson led her outside where a buggy waited. "Here you go, girl."

She took his hand as he helped her up into the seat. She scooted over so he could climb up and take the reins.

"I scolded that papa of yours with all the fiery heat of seven thousand suns, and your mama agreed with me." He slapped the reins over the horse. "Which put your papa into a terrible temper, but what could he do? His bride had made her sentiments known. So, your papa went out to find rings, I went to the church to set the priest in order, and your mama took her sweet time."

The image Mr. Albertson was painting made Annalee's heart squeeze with the joy of remembering her mother's ways. She'd always been a half-hour late to most things. Many an evening was spent with her father pacing the foyer of their home.

"And then that boy of *yours* was headin' off to do much the same, so I slowed him down when he come barrellin' into my lobby. As soon as I seen that look in his eye, I knew what was what." He turned the horse and buggy down a street that stretched to the right.

She realized they were headed to the church she'd been trying to get to earlier.

"Course, I was prepared to be lookin.'" Mr. Albertson let out a grunt.

Intrigued, she faced his profile. "You were prepared?"

"Your papa told me what to expect. When I first seen the two of ya, I wasn't too sure he was right. But then that boy nearly killed that other fella who took you, so I surmised that your boy was just a little stand-offish."

Stand-offish.

Was he?

She faced forward as she considered the possibility.

Perhaps he was. Hadn't he told her that her father had had to make him go to social events?

He was *shy*, she realized. She bit her lip as her heart swelled with love for him.

The church came into view.

"Somethin' else you may not know," Mr. Albertson said as he pulled the buggy to a stop.

She looked at him.

"I walked your mama down the aisle."

She gasped and covered her mouth with a hand.

The old man's eyes glinted with feeling. "And I'm gonna do the same for you."

How...beautiful. How *achingly* beautiful.

As Mr. Albertson climbed down, it took all of her control not to weep at the sweetness of what was happening. She was about to be married in the same church as her parents, and the man who'd been their witness and the person to escort her mother was going to do the same for Annalee. How...*perfect* this all was.

Her parents were gone. So was her brother.

A ceremony without them would've been sorrowful, but her papa had solved most of that problem. Because getting married here made her feel as if her family was with her. Her father had planned this entire thing.

Mr. Albertson appeared at her side and held up his hand. "Come on, then."

She swallowed and laid her palm in his.

Saint Martin Catholic Church was a small A-framed building made of stone. There was an alcove shading a set of oak doors.

Once inside, her focus went immediately to Ewan.

He straightened when he saw her and looked handsome as he waited near the altar with the priest.

"That's Father Gregory. Not the same man who married your parents, but he'll get the job done."

Annalee barely heard Mr. Albertson's words. She was drinking in the sight of her future husband.

He wore the suit he'd bought for the opera. He'd removed his hat, and his dark hair glinted in the setting rays of the sun shining through the stained glass windows flanking the church.

Slowly, Mr. Albertson led her down the aisle. With each step, her heart pounded harder, her smile got wider.

And Ewan...he smiled back.

And in his gaze was the promise of forever.

When she reached him, the priest began the ceremony, but she didn't take her eyes from Ewan.

At some point, Mr. Albertson handed her over to Ewan, and her hand was in his. His grip was strong and solid. Loyal. Trustworthy.

And her father's words from his last letter to her came rushing back. He'd told her he hoped it all worked out, and that if it did, he'd be thrilled and smiling down on her.

Oh...how *blessed* she was.

"HERE. SIT HERE."

Sheer bliss warmed Annalee completely through. Her cheeks hurt from the smile she'd worn for the last hour. Without a word, she did as her husband suggested, basking in his earnest need to care for her.

She sat down at the round table that had been placed in her room while they'd been at the church. A piping hot supper of roast and sides was waiting.

"Are you comfortable? Is this all right?"

"It's wonderful." Before he could move to the chair across from her, she grabbed his hand and stopped him.

Quiet descended. She gazed up at him, remembering his vows and the commitment they'd made to each other.

His expression went soft, and he sank to his knees. With a gentle hand, he stroked her cheek and jaw.

Love swelled inside her. "Ewan..."

"What is it?" he prodded gently.

This sweet, caring side of him was going to take some getting used to, but she was quite ready to enjoy it. "Tell me...why didn't you ever say anything before?"

He licked his lips, then gave her a soft smile. "Because you made me nervous."

She'd guessed as much, but it was so hard to believe. Not that she thought he was lying, but because he was so confident, courageous, and straight-forward. She let out a breath. "But I only seemed to irritate you. You never seemed nervous."

"That's because I teased you to keep distance between us." He brushed his palms down his thighs and exhaled. "I thought you were far above me, Annalee. Your father hired me when I knew next to nothing, but he told me I had good instincts about cattle, horses, the trail, the weather, and other things so he kept me as close to him as he did Ramsey. I was humbled. Did everything I could to make Jack proud.

"When I first saw you, out on the north pasture," he smiled at the memory, "you were sittin' underneath the windmill, reading, my heart leapt out of my chest and fell into your hands. It was the scariest moment of my life. You were like an angel, and I didn't think your father would ever want me for your husband.

"I couldn't risk anyone figuring out how I felt, so I teased you, kept myself apart from you as much as I could. And, truthfully, I didn't know how to talk to you anyway." He gave a rueful smile.

"I told you I'm not good with small talk, and I don't care much for dances or other social events. Jack was always dragging me to things, and after he made me foreman, he told me I was gonna have to get comfortable with conversation.

"I've been working on it, but it still makes my gut swim with nausea." He rubbed his stomach and shrugged. "Anyway," he cleared his throat, "despite my efforts to push you away, Jack still figured out how I felt. When he was sick, he called me to his bedside."

She inhaled sharply.

Ewan's gaze shone with compassion, with grief and sympathy. "He told me he knew how I felt, told me I was the man he wanted for you." He swallowed. "Told me that you..." He reached out and laid his hand over hers. "That you loved me, too."

She wasn't surprised. She should've realized her father had picked up on her feelings. "He was always intuitive."

Ewan nodded slowly. "But I didn't believe him. Or...I was scared to believe him." He withdrew an envelope from his coat pocket. "I want you to read this one now. It's the letter that was in the file with Jack's will."

She took it from him and with eager fingers, she withdrew the note.

Ewan,

You'll need to get her to Sinton. The next set of instructions will be at the depot with Bud. Go by horseback. When you're near a town, staying in hotels or eating in town is fine. Keep watch over her.

I'm giving this journey to you so you can fix things. You know what you need to do. Get it done.

Love her always.

Jack

"Oh, my goodness," she rasped, realizing she hadn't fully understood the trip her father had sent her on until now. "He didn't create this journey just for me. He did it for you, also." She looked at Ewan in surprise.

Slowly, he nodded. "Yes. He wanted you to experience the places you'd heard of, and he wanted me to take the time to repair my relationship with you and to...work up the damned courage to tell you how I felt."

Gratefulness washed through her, and she pressed the letter against her chest. "I'm so thankful he gave us this. I was so mad in the beginning, so hurt." She lowered the letter to her lap, then reached out a hand, wanting to touch him, but she stopped, uncertain.

He took her hand and threaded their fingers together.

The simple touch made her pulse race and her heart squeeze with overwhelming joy. Awe moved her. "I should've trusted that he knew what was best." Tears filled her eyes at the beauty that her life could now become.

"You're crying," Ewan said, slight alarm in his tone. "Why?"

She pressed trembling fingers to her lips and got control of herself. When her vision cleared, she let out a shuddering exhale. "It's just so beautiful, Ewan. While meeting Blackie, attending the opera, and all those other things were fun, nothing compares to becoming your wife."

Devotion and warmth shone in his eyes.

"After you called me Knobs—"

He drew breath, but she shook her head, stopping him.

"Let me finish. You don't need to explain or apologize."

He fell quiet.

"After you called me Knobs," she said again, continuing, "I decided you would never care for me, that I was too awkward for you, and I moved on. Or," she chuckled lightly, "I thought I did. I convinced myself that you weren't important to me. I only ended up fooling myself." She ran her gaze over his face, adoring him. "I've always loved you. It's always been you."

He made a noise of disbelief. "It's hard to believe that. I sure as hell don't know why you do, and God knows I don't deserve you."

"Oh, Ewan, please don't doubt your worth. Please don't set me higher than you. I—"

As he shook his head, he said, "You'll always be the most important person in my life. I've got you on a pedestal and you're gonna stay there."

She twitched her lips, wanting to argue. "I'm not perfect."

"Yes, you are."

"No, I'm not."

He grinned. "Are we fighting?"

She rolled her eyes. "If we are, it's the dumbest fight we've ever had."

He chuckled.

She sighed. "Just be logical and agree with me. No one is perfect."

With a lift of his brow, he said, "You don't think *I'm* perfect?"

She snorted.

"Huh. Only been my wife for five minutes and you're already insulting me."

She suppressed a grin. "Well...you're being ridiculously absurd. But I'll be using your irrational compliment of me to its full advantage."

"What's that mean?" His brown eyes gleamed with heat and mischief.

Oh, how handsome he was! And he was looking at her like he thought she was pretty. And he was her husband now. Her future was not going to be lonely any longer! "It means that anything I do, you'll have to like. Anything I say, you have to agree with."

He lifted an eyebrow. "Is that so?"

"Yep." She shrugged then batted her lashes at him. "I'm perfect."

He laughed. "Yeah, but you're also my wife."

She cocked her head. "And?"

"You have to obey me. So...if you say something not so perfect, or want to do something that's not the best idea, all I have to do is give you a better order and you have to follow it."

She gasped, feigning outrage. "I most certainly do not. I'm the boss."

"You think so? What happens if I take Wilton up on his offer, huh? You go where I go now. Think you can be the boss hundreds of miles away?"

She knew he wouldn't dare do that, but she still scowled at him. "I won't go with you."

He smiled with relish. "I'll just throw you over my shoulder and take you with me." He leaned in. "And nobody will stop me because I'm your husband."

Yes, he was. And he was smart. And kind. And capable. And gorgeous.

And his nearness was playing havoc with her will. Desire rose inside her, sending tingles all over her skin.

All the years of being around him and living without his love came rushing back. She couldn't take it. She threw her arms around him and kissed him.

He caught her, instantly enfolding her into his embrace.

Hunger flared, shooting into an unbearable inferno. He was her husband, and she was his wife. She was so happy, so relieved, so overjoyed. She never wanted to be apart from him again, and now she wouldn't have to.

He stood, taking her with him without any trouble. With her legs dangling, he carried her toward the bed, then set her on her feet. He broke their kiss. "You aren't hungry?"

She shook her head. Not for food, anyway.

His breath came hard and heavy. "I can make love to you?"

The hopeful yet gruff tone of his voice made her heart burn with love. "Please, Ewan. I need you."

Desire blazed in his eyes, and he took her mouth in a plundering kiss.

The yearning, the longing, was too much. They broke apart, each going for the other's clothing.

Feverishly, they undressed each other, their pants mingling with their hurried motions. Clothing hit the floor. Her dress, his coat. His vest, her corset.

Every bit came off until they were naked, but too needy for each other to take the time to look before he was tumbling her to the bed. They didn't even bother to pull back the blanket and sheets.

As he kissed her, he rocked against her.

She moaned in her throat and stroked his back with her palms. She had no real idea what to do, but her love for him, her desire for him spurred her on and she had no inhibitions.

His mouth moved down her neck, his hot breath making shivers spread over her skin. He nibbled and kissed her along her chest, then laved her nipple with his tongue.

And she went mindless. Helpless.

How could she have gone without him? Why had she been so blind to her feelings? She hated the years that she'd kept herself from him.

But now they were married. Gratefulness swamped her, and as he suckled her, she cried out her joy. He was everything. He was her whole world. She was going to be able to manage the Circle G without fear now that he was at her side forever.

His hands caressed her, stroking over her skin and making her move restlessly beneath him.

She had no control over her responses or reactions. She was in his thrall, but she was not afraid, because she trusted him implicitly.

His fingers slipped into the folds of her femininity, and she arched when his thumb brushed over the top. He rubbed and circled over the spot, slowly, sweetly, and she tossed her head fitfully on the pillows.

She called his name, begging for something she had no understanding of.

He rose up on his knees and spread her legs wide. "I can't wait, beautiful. I'm sorry."

His words confused her, but she didn't care what he meant. She just needed him.

He kissed her, open mouthed, his own desperation in his lips.

She felt him fill her, stretch her, and she hugged him tightly. Her fingers pressed into his back as her body welcomed him.

He pushed passed the barrier of her innocence and let out a low growl as he buried himself to the hilt.

She rejoiced inwardly that they were now one, that nothing would keep them apart.

He thrust into her, strong and steady. The bed shook with his motions, the posts clacking against the wall.

But she didn't care. Pleasure was building. Rapture was taking over. White heat was spreading through her and over her, reaching into her fingers and toes. She climbed higher and higher until she flew, and she cried out her amazement with abandon.

He followed immediately, calling her name and declaring his love. He collapsed on top of her, breathing heavily and shaking from the force of his release.

She held him, undone, awed. The beauty of their union was unexplainable, unbelievable. As she stroked her fingers through his hair, grateful tears pricked her eyes. "Ewan?"

"Yes?" he rasped into the crook of her shoulder.

"Is it always like this?"

After a moment, he shifted and raised up on an elbow. The lines of his face were laced with satisfaction. With his other hand, he brushed at the locks of hair along her temple. "I'm not sure. I've never made love with anyone else."

Amazement washed through her. "You haven't?"

He shook his head. "Couldn't. I loved you too much."

Her love for him burst inside her, more glorious than the flight he'd just given her. "Oh, Ewan."

"But we'll make our lives exactly what we want, and there's nothing that says it can't always be like the first time. We have each other, and that's all we need."

She cupped his cheek as the tears from only moments ago now slid down her temples. "I'm going to thank God for you every day. You're a blessing, Ewan."

A grin played at his lips. "I've gone from a consistent pain to a blessing, huh?" He smiled. "Should've married you sooner."

She laughed in delight, then he set his lips to hers and desire built once more.

Epilogue

Yellow Rose Hall
Houston, Texas
One month later

Ewan gritted his teeth, keeping his mouth shut as Mrs. Jolly Ackers tried to talk Annalee out of cross-breeding the Circle G's steers with Vaughn's and Wilton's stock. How his wife could be patient and calm, he didn't know. Of course, he hated shindigs like this.

Well, to be fair, he hated *all* social functions. At least this conference of cattle barons was easier to stomach since they were mostly talking about ranching and all its trappings.

To keep from arguing with Mrs. Ackers who still harped about Wilton's lack of organizational skills, Ewan allowed the goings on of the rest of the assembly to distract him.

Seventy tables dressed with gleaming white linen and sparkling crystal held the remnants of a succulent meal of roasted duck and savory sides. Men in three-piece suits and Stetsons, and women in vibrant silk or satin dresses stood about the space, or still sat in the gold rimmed chairs, waiting for the orchestra in the adjacent chamber to start playing.

The low hum of conversation reverberated through the dining hall, slightly muffled by the shining mahogany paneling and plush carpeting. Crystal chandeliers hung overhead, while electronic sconces made of brass helped bathe the room in a warm glow. Despite the season, yellow roses were in vases atop pedestals placed along the outskirts of the room.

It had been a fine supper. Thankfully, Vaughn, Wilton and their wives had been at Ewan's and Annalee's table, and the conversation had been tolerable. Though Vaughn had monopolized most of it.

Their stay had comprised two days of meetings and a parade of vendors hawking the newest products for making ranching easier. There had been demonstrations in the arena of some of the machinery.

Annalee was very interested in delving into the strides made with equipment that would make bathing cattle easier. Ewan had agreed with her.

The condescending tone of Mrs. Ackers drew Ewan's focus.

"Annalee, dear," the woman was saying, "you've only been at this for one month, and this is your first conference. I've been coming to these since my husband started the Bar A and have learned so much more. You must think about this more carefully. Gregory Vaughn and Beau Wilton are a pair of impulsive idiots. They don't even buy their feed from Stracks in San Antonio and—"

"Jolly," Annalee interrupted firmly but nicely, "I don't buy my feed from Stracks either, and you know the Circle G has always had extremely healthy herds."

"Yes, but—"

"This is a venture I've researched extensively for the last several weeks, and I'm intrigued by the even hardier herd it could create." Annalee reached out and patted the woman's shoulder.

Mrs. Ackers' lips pinched in irritation.

"Don't fret," Annalee continued. "Your concern is comforting, but as you can plainly see, since he hasn't left my side all night and has heard every word you've said, the best cowboy in the state hasn't once agreed with you. And he hasn't *dis*agreed with me."

Mrs. Ackers tossed her head, her gray locks swishing, and scoffed. "He's your husband."

"And quite capable of telling me when he thinks I'm making a foolish decision." Annalee chuckled and looked up at him.

He smiled at her, recalling their years of fights just as he knew she was doing.

"Believe me," his wife went on, "he would not stay quiet if he thought I was wrong. Especially since the Circle G is the future for any children the Lord might bless us with."

"Well," Mrs. Ackers huffed, then turned her head away from them. "Ah, I see my husband is calling me to his side. I shall leave you. Good luck to you, Annalee."

"Thank you, Jolly."

The woman turned and walked so briskly, her silk train snapped with vigor.

Annalee chuckled as Mrs. Ackers left them. "People have been so ready with their advice, don't you think?"

Ewan let out a breath of frustration. "I didn't realize how annoying it was gonna be. I never came to these with Jack. I suspect he had to field a lot of judgments about the decisions he was making."

"Yes, well, I think I'm holding up, don't you?"

He quirked a grin at her, fondness sweeping through him. "You're doing much better than me. Took all my control not to holler at that woman."

Annalee slipped her fingers around the crook of his elbow. "She means well."

He made a noise of disagreement.

Just then the music struck up from the ballroom next door. The sound of a string orchestra swelled through the open double doors, and Annalee tightened her grip on his arm. "Oh, wonderful! The dancing is about to start."

Her excitement had her sliding her hand down his arm to slip her fingers between his. With a radiant smile at him, she tugged him toward the music.

He let himself be led, admiring the view as he followed. Her cream silk dress curved over her hips and fell in ripples down her legs. The square neckline showed her delicate collar bones and a hint of her breasts. Her raven tresses were piled on her head in glossy ringlets that tickled her bare neck. But the sweetest part of her appearance was the embellishment of flowers, Texas Green Eyes, that had been stitched along the neckline and trailed down over the line of her waist and her right hip.

She was dazzling. Startling.

They reached the dance floor, and he immediately swept her into the waltz, smiling down at her as desire rose inside him entwining with the love and devotion continuously beating in his heart.

She gazed up at him with that adoring twinkle in her eye that he planned to keep there always.

"I love you," he told her.

She smiled and winked at him.

He chuckled. "I'm only gonna dance with you tonight."

"And why is that?" she teased.

She knew why, so he didn't answer. He just led her through the steps, keeping his eyes on her.

"Is it because you don't make small talk?"

Again, he didn't respond. He quirked a grin at her.

"Or maybe it's because you're afraid you'll step on someone's toes."

He shook his head at her teasing but ignored it otherwise.

"Or maybe..." she drew out her thought and gave him a look filled with desire, "you only want to be in *my* arms."

He pulled her in closer and felt his heart expand with love. "You finally got it right."

She didn't respond but continued to look at him with nothing short of adoration.

They fell silent as they waltzed, keeping their gazes locked on each other.

This was his. This life that had been given to him for reasons he couldn't identify. But he wouldn't take it for granted ever.

Annlee was his wife.
The spunky cowgirl.
The woman cattle baron.
Miss Green Eyes.

About the Author

Award-winning author Kara O'Neal is a teacher and lives in Texas with her husband and three children. She writes stories with strong family ties, lots of romance and guaranteed happy endings! Please visit her at www.karaoneal.com[1].

---

1. http://www.karaoneal.com

Don't miss out!

Visit the website below and you can sign up to receive emails whenever Kara O'Neal publishes a new book. There's no charge and no obligation.

https://books2read.com/r/B-A-VUGK-ZVPBD

Connecting independent readers to independent writers.

Also by Kara O'Neal

Gamblers & Gunslingers
Katie's Gamble
Felicity's Fortune
Cora Lee's Wager
Olivia's Treasure
Joetta's Legacy
Everleigh's Game

Texas Brides of Pike's Run
Saving Sarah
Welcome Home
The Sheriff's Gift
The Cowboy's Charms
The Miller Brides
The Soldier's Love
Love's Promise
Love's Redemption
The Editor's Kisses
The Ranger's Vow
The Cowboy's Embrace
Destiny's Secrets
Mr. Pierce's Hero

The Christmas Bride
Maggie's Song
The Inventor's Heart
The Deputy's Damsel
An Unacceptable Wife
The Cowboy's Bride
The Princess's Knight
Sunshine's Welcome
Forever Home

Wildflowers of Texas
Miss Green Eyes

Watch for more at www.karaoneal.com.

About the Author

Award-winning author, Kara O'Neal is a teacher and lives in Texas with her husband and three children. She writes stories with strong family ties, lots of romance and guaranteed happy endings! Visit her at www.karaoneal.com.

Read more at www.karaoneal.com.